DEMONS

"Nameless Detective" Mysteries

by BILL PRONZINI

DEMONS

EPITAPHS

QUARRY

BREAKDOWN

JACKPOT

SHACKLES

DEADFALL

BONES

DOUBLE (*with Marcia Muller*)

NIGHTSHADES

QUICKSILVER

CASEFILE (*collection*)

BINDLESTIFF

DRAGONFIRE

SCATTERSHOT

HOODWINK

LABYRINTH

TWOSPOT (*with Collin Wilcox*)

BLOWBACK

UNDERCURRENT

THE VANISHED

THE SNATCH

DEMONS

A "Nameless Detective" Mystery

by

BILL PRONZINI

Delacorte Press

1315 9346

Published by
Delacorte Press
Bantam Doubleday Dell Publishing Group, Inc.
1540 Broadway
New York, New York 10036

Library of Congress Cataloging in Publication Data

Pronzini, Bill.
    Demons : a "nameless detective" mystery / by Bill Pronzini.
        p.   cm.
    ISBN 0-385-30505-2 : $19.95
    I. Title.
    PS3566.R67D46   1993
    813'.54—dc20   92-40280
                                                     CIP

Manufactured in the United States of America

Published simultaneously in Canada

September 1993

10 9 8 7 6 5 4 3 2 1

BVG

For my new in-laws:
Kathryn, Lois, and Henry Muller
and
Carol and Karl Brandt

Yes, there is a devil,
Of that there is no doubt.
But is he trying to get in us,
Or is he trying to get out?

—OLD RHYME

Chapter 1

I SAID, "I don't like divorce work, Joe. You know that. The only time I'll do it is when I need money. And right now I don't need money."

"Kay doesn't want a divorce," DeFalco said.

"Same kind of dirty job."

"You won't have to take photos or make tapes or anything like that. Find out who the woman is, that's essentially it."

"Essentially?"

"Well, there is a minor complication."

"There are always complications, and they're usually not so minor. What's this one?"

"I'd better let her tell you."

"Uh-huh. So I find out the woman's identity—then what? Kay confronts her?"

"She's not violent, if that's what you're thinking."

I sighed. "Talk it over woman-to-woman, appeal to the dolly's sense of decency and fair play. Right?"

"Something like that."

"And what if the girlfriend won't give him up?"

"Kay's at the end of her rope. If she can't put an end to the affair herself, she'll walk."

"Yeah."

"No, she will. You don't know her; I do."

I thought: Nobody knows anybody, not really. We don't even know ourselves. But I didn't say it.

DeFalco sat slouched in the client's chair across my desk, watching me with his shrewd reporter's eyes. He doesn't look like a newspaperman; nor, for that matter, does he look Italian. He looks like Pat O'Brien playing Father Jerry in *Angels with Dirty Faces*. People tell him things they wouldn't tell anybody else. Friends also turn to him for favors in a time of need. And when that happens, Joe being lazy and something of a buck-passer, his first inclination is to dump the whole thing, favor included, into the lap of another friend. In this case, me.

"Well?" he said.

"No," I said.

"Come on, she's a nice lady. No bull. I've known her since we were radicals together at Berkeley."

"You were never a radical."

"In spirit I was," he said. "Be a mensch, will you? She's hurting, bad, and she needs help and there's nothing much I can do for her. It's your kind of work."

"Sure it is."

"You picked the profession, pal. Nobody forced you to become a private eye."

I sighed again. If this were a comic strip—and my life felt like one sometimes—one of those word balloons would come out of my ear in the next panel and the word printed in it would be SUCKER! I said, "All right. I'll talk to her. No promises beyond that."

He gave me his wise Pat O'Brien smile along with Kay Runyon's address and telephone number. I wasn't kidding *him,* the smile said. It also said I wasn't kidding myself and we both knew it, didn't we? Right on both counts, the smug bastard.

At the door he paused and took a look around the half-empty loft, the way he had when he'd first come in. Don't say it, Joe, I thought; you got this far without saying anything, just let it go. But he didn't let it go, not my old pal, Mr. Sensitive. He said, "This place is too big for a one-man operation. You ought to take in another partner. Or get yourself a smaller layout."

I kept my mouth shut.

"Any plans along those lines?"

"No," I said.

"Think about it," he said. Then he said, "You hear from Eberhardt since he moved out?"

This time, teeth clenched, I shook my head.

"Me neither. I guess he's cut off a lot of his old friends."

No comment.

"I hear he's not doing too well. That what you hear?"

No comment, damn it.

"Well, he made his own bed," DeFalco said. "Still, I'd hate to see him go down the tubes. You'd take him back, wouldn't you? If he can't hack it on his own and comes begging?"

Enough. "Get out of here," I said. "Go rake some muck at city hall."

"You don't want to talk about it, huh? Eberhardt?"

"Good-bye, Joe."

"Sure, I know how you feel. I'm on your side. Call me after you talk to Kay."

"Good-bye, Joe."

He went. And a little while later, so did I.

KAY RUNYON and her allegedly philandering husband lived in Ashbury Heights, a little pocket of affluence on the hill above the Haight-Ashbury. Old money up there—nervous money in the late sixties, when the Haight had been the center of the Flower Power, free love, let's-all-get-stoned counterculture. The citizens of the Heights had survived the hippies with their property values intact, and were now in the process of surviving the drug-infested, homeless-dominated new Haight scene. Still nervous

about the shape of things below, no doubt, but reasonably confident in the long view. If you live high enough on the hill, any
hill, and you're wary and well insulated, you can survive anything the rabble does down in the bottoms. That's the theory,
anyway, that the great visionaries in Washington had been tacitly
propounding for a dozen years. The gospel according to St. Ron-
ald and St. George.

The Runyon house was a tall, narrow Mediterranean:
stucco-faced, painted a creamy silver-gray, with cathedral-style
windows of leaded glass and black wrought-iron balconies and
trim. A double tier of brick steps led up onto a side porch from
the street—fifteen steps in each tier. High, high on the hill. I
wondered what Victor Runyon did for a living, to afford this kind
of home. Or, not to be sexist, what Kay Runyon did. DeFalco
hadn't told me which of them controlled the family purse strings,
or where the money in the purse came from.

The front door opened before I was halfway up the second
tier and Kay Runyon came out to greet me. I'd called her before
leaving the office—a thirty-second conversation to determine
that she was home and available for a conference right away. She
had sounded tense on the phone and she looked tense in person:
woman on the edge, and trying so hard not to show it that her
balance was all the more precarious. She was about forty, too
thin in baggy slacks and a white velour pullover, as if she might
be anorectic; hair a sandy blond, worn shoulder-length in one of
those fluffy, in-curving styles; large gray eyes that would have
been striking except for the smudges under them and the pain in
their depths. Twenty years ago she'd have had suitors of all
shapes, sizes, and ages beating down her door. Now, what should
have been an equally potent mature beauty was blurred, marred
by the effects of strain and emotional upheaval.

She subjected me to an intense five-second scrutiny of her
own, and the impression she got seemed to reassure her. She
shook my hand, said, "Thank you for coming, I really do appreciate it," and ushered me into a big, angular living room. Everything in there was either orange or white or a combination of the

two colors, including some oddly fuzzy impressionistic paintings on the wall and such accoutrements as vases, coasters, a table lighter, and ashtrays. There was plenty of light—from a chandelier and two table lamps, as well as from the sunny August day outside—and the effect should have been warm and cheery. Not for me, though. All that orange and white made me cold because it reminded me of a Dreamsicle, one of my generation's kid treats: orange-flavored ice on the outside, vanilla ice cream on the inside. My old man loved Dreamsicles—just a big overgrown kid himself—and was always trying to get me to eat them, couldn't understand why I kept refusing. Once, when I turned one down, he knocked me flat and stood over me shaking it, splattering me with cold melting orange and white, telling me what an ungrateful little shit I was. Some guy, my old man. Every boy's ideal pop.

Kay Runyon and I sat on white chairs with orange cushions. She lit a cigarette, began to smoke it in quick little drags. It was very quiet in the house, so quiet you could hear the faint hiss of the tobacco igniting each time she inhaled.

Pretty soon she said, "I don't know where to start."

"Wherever it's easiest for you."

"Well . . . Joe told you my problem. Joe DeFalco."

"Yes."

"That my husband is having an affair."

"Yes."

"It's . . . no, it's *not* just an affair. I could deal with it if that's all it was."

"Have you had to before? Deal with that kind of thing?"

"You mean is Vic a habitual cheat? No. As far as I know he was faithful to me for nearly nineteen years. That's one of the things that makes all this so crazy, so . . ." She shook her head, jabbed out the remains of her weed in an orange clamshell ashtray, and immediately lit another.

"You think he's in love with this woman, then?"

"No," Kay Runyon said. "I think he's obsessed with her."

"Obsessed?"

"I know that sounds melodramatic, but it's the literal truth. He's not just sleeping with her, he's not just infatuated with her . . . he's pathologically obsessed with her."

"If you could be more specific . . ."

"He isn't the same man since it started. Not at *all* the same man. He doesn't act or interact the same—I'm sure he doesn't think the same. It's as if he's with her even when he's here with me, as if nothing else—me, our son, our lives together, his job, none of it—is vital to him anymore."

"How long has he been this way?"

"The relationship started eight or nine months ago, some-time before Christmas. At least that's when I first suspected he was seeing someone. The obsession . . . four months or so. But I suppose it had been building all along."

The length of time surprised me a little. "And he hasn't asked you for a divorce?"

"No. I kept expecting it, dreading it . . . but no. I suppose it's because she's married, too, and doesn't want to or can't get out."

That was one explanation. I could think of a couple of others, both fear-related, but I didn't share them with her. I asked, "Have you confronted him about the affair?"

"I tried. It was . . . bizarre."

"How so?"

"He wouldn't admit or deny it," she said. "Wouldn't talk about it at all. He just . . . retreated. Into himself, like a turtle pulling its head into its shell. My God, it was like trying to talk to a stranger, a retarded person. There was just no connection." She shivered, jabbed out her second cigarette, hugged herself. The lower parts of her arms, bare beneath the half-rolled pullover sleeves, were riddled with goose bumps. "No connection," she said again.

"The affair started sometime before Christmas, you said. Do you have any idea where or how?"

"No. She's someone he met through his work, I think. He's not a social animal. I mean he doesn't sit in bars by himself, doesn't have the kind of male friends who go prowling in packs. Doesn't have many friends at all, in fact. Until eight months ago he was a family man and a workaholic.''

"What kind of work does he do?''

"He's an architect. Private homes, mainly. He's quite well known, quite successful.'' There was pride in her voice; even after all the pain he'd caused her, she was still proud of him. "Not just in the city or Bay Area—all over the state.''

"A workaholic, you said. Would you describe him as driven?''

"Yes. He's that kind of man. Not such a long step from work obsession to woman obsession, if that's what you're thinking.''

"Something like that. Does he do much traveling?''

"Some. Quite a lot in the past several months—to be with her, I'm sure.''

"Away for long periods of time?''

"Three or four days at the most. But I don't think he met her while he was away. I think he met her right here in the city. I think she lives here or in a town close by.''

"What makes you believe that?''

"Well, in the first place he was home most of November— just one overnight consultancy trip to L.A.—and all of December. In the second place . . . lately, when he's not out of town, he goes to see her two or three nights a week.''

"Spends the entire night with her?''

"No. At least he hasn't gone that far yet. He comes home, but not until late—midnight or after. Goes straight to her from his office, or meets her somewhere, or whatever.'' Another head-shake. "I don't want to know that part of it. What they do when they're alone . . . the damn details.''

"He doesn't call you on those nights, make excuses?''

"No. If he's not here by six-thirty, then I know it's one of his nights with . . .'' Emotion drowned the rest of the sentence. I watched her struggle against it, try to hide it by lighting yet another coffin nail.

In one of the other rooms a telephone rang.

Kay Runyon's head jerked a little; she said, "My God," and got abruptly to her feet. But she didn't go anywhere, just stood there rigidly listening to the phone ring three more times. Then she said, "Excuse me, please," without looking at me, and went out of there at a half run, trailing cigarette smoke.

The chair cushion was hard on my backside; I squirmed on it, fighting off the urge to get up and walk around. If I did that I would probably keep right on walking out the door, out of the troubled lives of Kay and Victor Runyon. This wasn't my kind of case—I *hated* this kind of case. DeFalco and his goddamn favors.

From the other room the sound of her voice came faintly. Too faintly for me to make out the words, but the harsh overtones of anger came through. The conversation didn't last long; she was back in not much more than a minute. It hadn't been a good call for her. Her face was paler and she seemed shaky now. When she sat down again her knees seemed to bend too quickly, so that she half collapsed into the chair.

"Nedra," she said, as if she were uttering an obscenity.

". . . I'm sorry?"

"That's her name, the bitch."

"Whose name?"

"Vic's obsession, the woman he's fucking."

"You mean she just telephoned you—?"

"No, no. That was him again, the man who keeps calling."

"What man?"

"I don't know."

"Mrs. Runyon, you're not making sense to me. Let's back up a little here. You told Joe DeFalco you had no idea who the woman is, you led me to believe the same thing, and now you say her name is Nedra."

"That's all I know about her, her first name."

"Who told you that? Your husband?"

"No. The man who keeps calling."

"Why does he keep calling?"

"To harass Vic, but he's driving *me* crazy too."

"Harass him how?"

"He wants Vic to stay away from her. Nedra. My God, it's the same thing *I* want. I've tried to tell him that but he won't talk to me, he won't listen to me."

DeFalco's "minor complication." I asked, "How long has this been going on? These anonymous calls?"

"A couple of weeks."

"How often? Every day?"

"Almost. Sometimes once or twice a day."

"If he won't talk to you, how did you hear the name Nedra?"

"It was the first time he called . . . the first time I know about. Vic was home, here in the house, and I was in my studio out back, and he and I happened to pick up at the same time. Vic said hello before I could, and this man's voice said, 'Stay away from Nedra, you son of a bitch, if you know what's good for you.' "

"A voice you'd never heard before?"

"Never."

"What did your husband say?"

"Nothing. He didn't have time. The man called him another name, much worse, and hung up."

"Did you ask Vic who he is?"

"Of course. He withdrew again."

"But you think he knows the man's identity?"

"Oh, he knows. He must know. I'm terrified that . . ."

"What? The caller will make good on his threat?"

"Yes. This is a crazy world, full of crazy people. He has to be unstable, to make all those calls. Who knows what he might do?"

She was right, but I didn't voice my agreement. I didn't say anything.

"That's one of the reasons I have to know who Nedra is," Kay Runyon said. "You see? Who she is and who the man is. Then I can talk to her—to him, too, if necessary—face-to-face.

Not just for my sake, for Vic's and for our son's. You do under-stand?''

"I understand that what's brewing here is pretty volatile, Mrs. Runyon—"

"Yes. Exactly.''

"—and that you could make it worse by becoming person-ally involved with Nedra and this champion of hers.''

"Are you saying it's better I don't know who they are? That I just let things go along as they have?''

"No. I'm advising caution, that's all.''

"I intend to be cautious. Very. But I have to know. I'm *going* to know, one way or another. If you won't help me—''

She broke off because there were running footsteps on the stairs outside, then heavy on the porch. A key rattled; the front door opened and then banged shut. A young male voice called, "Mom? You here?''

"In the living room, Matt.''

A teenage version of Kay Runyon appeared in the doorway. He was sixteen or seventeen, his blond hair worn in a tight bristle cut, his clothing a pair of rumpled cords and one of those blue-and-white long-sleeved sweatshirts baseball players wear. He looked like a ballplayer: lean, rangy, long-armed, and strong. In one hand he carried a plastic sack tied off at the top and full of something that couldn't be very heavy.

"I got the lint,'' he said. "You want it in . . . oh.''

He'd spotted me, and it worked an immediate transforma-tion on him. He froze in place, his body tensing.

Kay Runyon said, "It's all right, Matt. This man's here to help us.'' She made introductions, and her son—Matthew, she said formally—unbent enough to come over and shake my hand, quick and hard. But the tenseness remained in him, and he had nothing to say to me. He turned back to his mother, jiggling the sack.

"You want me to put this stuff in the studio?''

"Yes. Go ahead, we're almost finished here.''

He nodded and went out without looking at me again.

I said, "Lint?"

"Dryer lint. There are two Laundromats in the area that save it for me. Matt collects it when they have a sackful."

"What do you use it for?"

"Didn't Joe tell you? I'm an artist—I do representational and impressionistic paintings, using dryer lint as a central ingredient."

"Uh, I see."

Ghost of a smile. "It's an established modern technique," she said. "That's one of my better efforts on the wall behind you."

I looked. Furry geometrical designs arranged on a snowy white field, none of them quite touching one another, each in a slightly different shade of orange. "It's very good," I said. I had no idea if it was good or not; what I know about art you could hide in a spoonful of dryer lint.

"Thank you."

One of those little awkward silences then, the kind that develop between strangers in unrelaxed circumstances. Thick quiet had reclaimed the house. I still wanted to get up and walk out, but I didn't do it.

"He knows, of course," Kay Runyon said abruptly.

"Matt?"

"Yes. What's going on with his father, the phone calls, all of it. We don't have secrets in this house. Didn't used to have secrets, anyway."

Another small silence. She looked at me steadily, waiting, as tense now as her son had been.

It's all right, Matt. This man's here to help us.

Well, somebody had to, right? And what difference did it make to me, really, who paid my fees and what kind of work I did as long as it was worthwhile. I got out my notebook.

TWENTY MINUTES LATER, out in the car, I didn't feel quite so nobly philosophical. I thought: Obsessive affair, harassing phone calls, not-so-veiled threats, people in pain living on the edge—a situation simmering with all sorts of explosive possibilities. Plus a Dreamsicle living room and paintings made with dryer lint. I must be crazy to get mixed up in a thing like this.

Right.

Just another day in the asylum . . .

Chapter **2**

AT FIVE-FIFTEEN that evening I was legally parked at a meter on Second Street, between Brannan and Townsend. It had taken me twenty-five minutes of cruising around, and a little fast maneuvering to ace out an irate woman in a Cadillac who also wanted the space—and at that I considered myself fortunate. I'd been prepared to do a lot of hovering and/or park illegally to maintain surveillance on the parking garage just down the block. The garage was where Victor Runyon kept his car—a maroon '91 BMW, his wife had told me—while he was in his office around the corner on Brannan.

This was an area of the city that had changed radically over the past couple of decades. Once its streets and narrow alleys and old brick and stone and wood buildings had been home to light industry, to ship's chandleries and marine supply outfits that catered to San Francisco's now-moribund shipping trade. In those days it had been known as South of the Slot, "slot" being old-timer's parlance for Market Street. As the port declined, so did the district. In the sixties and early seventies, some of the industrial outfits had closed down or moved out, and the area had degenerated into an adjunct to Skid Row: flophouses, cheap bars, empty buildings and warehouses, heavy drug use in and around South Park. Then the city fathers, in a rare exercise of good judgment, had stepped in and started an aggressive urban renewal program; and farsighted developers, who had correctly predicted the real estate boom of the mid-seventies, had bought up property and begun tearing down some of the worst of the derelicts and putting up new buildings, and refurbishing the "quaint" old brick warehouses into gentrified office and showroom space. Clothiers and people involved in the interior design trade moved in; so did architects and artists and food and entertainment entrepreneurs. Now what you had was a burgeoning San Francisco version of New York's SoHo, replete with a similar trendy name: SoMa, short for South of Market. By day it was a diverse "mixed-use" jumble of printing outfits, auto repair shops, social service agencies, pawnshops, transient hotels and senior citizens' residences peacefully coexisting with art galleries, factory-outlet clothing and jewelry stores, gourmet food and wine shops, and a variety of white-collar offices. By night it was a racy Bohemian blend of restaurants, comedy clubs, and gay leather bars and straight dancing clubs along Folsom Street's so-called Miracle Mile.

I'm not a big advocate of change, but in this case I approved of the South of Market metamorphosis. I could remember the good old days when the area had had a crusty seaman's flavor, but I could also remember the bad old days when it had been the domain of crumbling buildings and crumbling humanity. Mindless change—the tearing down of the functional old in favor of the glittery, too-often impermanent new—is one thing; reclamation and self-preservation by surgery is another. South of the Slot was dead. Long live SoMa.

The streets were crowded at the moment, with people leaving the offices and galleries and showrooms for the day. I couldn't have picked Victor Runyon out of the crowd streaming past, even though his wife had provided me with a clear color photo of him; but I didn't have to try. He rarely left his office until five-thirty and usually not until six, she'd told me—a pattern he had evidently maintained even while in the throes of his affair with Nedra. Maybe so, but where stakeouts are concerned I prefer not to leave anything to chance. While hunting this parking space I'd called his office from my mobile phone, feigning a wrong number. He was there.

I took his photo out again and had another look at it. Handsome guy: fair-skinned, though with brown hair that was on the curly side; ascetic features, soft mouth, gentle brown eyes under abnormally long lashes. There was intelligence and sensitivity in the face, but there was also weakness. I wondered again what went on inside the head of a man like him; how, if his wife was right about him, he could have emotionally paralyzed himself. I understood obsessive-compulsive behavior well enough; I had a mild case of it myself, where my job was concerned. But I recognized the symptoms when they appeared, had always been able to control them. A man who was so weak as to allow an obsession to rule his emotions and then to undermine the foundations of his life was alien to me.

Five-thirty. The crowds and the traffic on Townsend and on Second were thinning. It had been a clear, cool day, and now the sunlight was softening into a mellow gold where it lay in angles and patches on the streets and against buildings. Down along the Embarcadero, now that the remains of the earthquake-damaged Embarcadero Freeway had finally been torn down, that soft gold light on the bay, on the old pier sheds and the restored eminence of the Ferry Building, would be making the tourists sing the city's praises. The coming night would be nice, too, one where lights and colors stand out in sharp relief against a darkness that seems as hard as black glass. From the balcony of Kerry's apartment in Diamond Heights, you'd have a miles-wide view as far east as Mount Diablo.

That was where I wanted to be tonight, up there with Kerry. I hadn't seen much of her lately and I was lonesome. But given the fact that she'd been in conference when I called Bates and Carpenter shortly before five, and her secretary had said she had another meeting scheduled for six, my prospects were poor. Creative director for a small but aggressive ad agency is more than a full-time job; it's a commitment that takes precedence over just about everything, including a normal personal life. I resented that, but I couldn't argue with it. It was the same sort of commitment I'd made to my own profession a long time ago. Workaholics, Kerry and me. Chafing at the harness sometimes, sure, but knowing we wouldn't be worth a damn unless we were wearing it.

Six o'clock coming up. Not too many pedestrians now and I paid closer attention to the ones that passed on this side of the street, approaching from Brannan. Victor Runyon finally showed at three minutes after the hour: alone, walking briskly with a stiff-backed posture, eyes straight ahead. Tan gabardine suit, no tie, light tan trench coat unbuttoned and flapping like wings in the thin evening breeze. I shifted on the seat to get a better look at him as he passed. No expression on his ascetic face. Man with things on his mind . . . man with a purpose for tonight? I watched him enter the parking garage; then I started the car and backed up a little, to make sure I could get out of the space easily when the time came.

It was not long before the maroon BMW appeared. Runyon was at the wheel; I could see him clearly when he braked before turning south toward Townsend. I eased out behind him.

West on Townsend, driving neither fast nor slow, changing lanes only when it was necessary. I dropped back just far enough to be certain I could make every light he did. Right on Duboce, Duboce to Market, up Market to Twin Peaks. If he'd been going home to Ashbury Heights he'd have then taken Divisadero, or maybe Clayton halfway up; he didn't turn on either street.

I moved up closer to him as we neared the top of Market, where it becomes Portola Drive. Traffic was heavy and I didn't want to lose him. He had no idea he was being followed; when you've been at the game as long as I have, you can tell when a subject is suspicious. Man with a purpose, all right—totally focused on getting to where he was headed. I could ride his bumper all the way, I thought, and still he wouldn't have a clue that I was there.

Beyond the big intersection at O'Shaughnessy, he turned left and swung around and back into the Tower shopping center. Going after groceries or liquor, maybe . . . but I was wrong about that. He parked in front of a florist shop, hurried inside while I hovered illegally in the vicinity, and reappeared a few minutes later with two huge, green-paper-wrapped bouquets of flowers.

From the shopping center he drove back onto Portola and then turned downhill past the Youth Guidance Center and Laguna Honda Hospital. Another turn on Clarendon, a broad avenue that winds along the south side of Mount Sutro above one of the city's reservoirs. Near the top of Clarendon he swung left into the moderately expensive residential district called Forest Hill.

The streets up there were narrow and twisty, all the houses built along the west sides to take advantage of sweeping views of the ocean, the hills and the flatlands of the city's western perimeter. The land on the right sides was too steep to build on; thick forest, dominated by eucalyptus, provided a rustic backdrop and the false illusion of country privacy. Attractive part of San Francisco to call home, as long as you didn't subscribe to the theory that a catastrophic earthquake was going to hammer this old town someday. The houses—smallish, brick or stucco over wood, each with a two-car garage—were all on steep ground, and while there was bedrock up here, there was also plenty of loose topsoil; and too many homes had been built on wooden pilings instead of on concrete foundations dug into the hillside. A big enough shake, centered on the San Andreas Fault nearby, and everything on this hill could conceivably wind up in one disastrous heap on the flats below.

Crestmont was the street Runyon wanted, the dead-end section beyond Devonshire. Secluded little pocket here, very woodsy, hidden away from the eyes and minds of 99 percent of the population. The houses and lots were larger and not quite as uniformly nondescript: wood-shingled or angularly modernistic with too much glass, set back far enough from the street so that most had small fenced-in decks or gardens in front.

There was parking along the right side of the street, where the woods crowded down close against brick and concrete retaining walls. Runyon slowed, pulled his BMW to the curb opposite a wood-shingled house stained a dark red. I drove on past him without slowing down and without looking his way. At the circle where the street dead-ended I turned around and came back far enough to see him getting out of his car with the two bouquets of flowers. Then I parked, too, about fifty yards away.

The dark-red house was his final destination. He opened a gate in the high wooden fence in front, using a key, and disappeared through it. I sat quiet for five minutes; he didn't come back out. I quit the car then and walked over there, taking my time, like a man enjoying a casual stroll in his own neighborhood.

The house didn't look large from the street, but it was built on two levels. A wooden staircase ran down along the north side, to a landing and a door that would open into the lower level. Through the gap there that separated the red house from its northside neighbor, I could see Ocean Beach and the Pacific beyond; the westering sun made the water look like something out of a fiery biblical prophecy. The fence in front was too high to see over, but there were chinks between the gate boards that gave me glimpses of potted shrubs, an agave cactus in a wooden tub, a glass-topped table. Affixed to the gate were three block numerals made out of redwood: 770.

On the south side of the fence there was a driveway that led into a smallish two-car garage. I paused there, pretended to stretch, and tried to determine if the garage was occupied. Couldn't do it; the angle was wrong and the door was windowless. Not that it mattered much either way.

I walked most of the distance to Devonshire, still taking my time. Nothing had changed at the red house when I came back past it. I sat in the car for another five minutes, to make the surveillance a full half-hour in length. Victor Runyon was still inside when I finally went away from there.

OFFICES ARE LONELY PLACES at night. Mine in particular: big, half-empty loft in an old building on O'Farrell that is deserted after five-thirty, the other two tenants being the Slim-Taper Shirt Company on the second floor and Martin Quon's Bay City Realtors on the ground floor. Ghosts walk here after dark—the ghosts of past cases and a friendship and partnership suddenly and inexplicably dead four months ago. I don't come to the office at night much since Eberhardt walked out on me; I don't like the ghosts or the emptiness. But tonight I had a reason, and I was not going to hang around long enough for the after-hours atmosphere to depress me.

Maybe DeFalco's right, I thought as I switched on my desk lamp. Maybe I ought to get out of here, rent a smaller, cheerier space in a better neighborhood. There was nothing keeping me in this gloomy garret except inertia. Eberhardt wasn't coming back; even if he failed with his own agency, his pride wouldn't let him. And my pride wouldn't let me, either. Too much hurt, too much damage that couldn't be undone. Long, close friendships die hard; but once they're dead, they're better off buried for good.

I dragged out my copy of the reverse city directory. Number 770 Crestmont was owned by Nedra Adams Merchant—sole ownership, no other property holder listed. Her occupation was given as graphics designer. She was also the sole occupant of the house, at least insofar as the city census was concerned.

Nedra. Nedra Adams Merchant. Nice euphonious name. Nice person, too, even though she happened to be screwing a married man? Be a relief for all concerned if it turned out that way.

I looked up her name in the Yellow Pages, under *Graphics Designers*. No listing. Operated her company under another name, or worked for somebody else. Or had some other source of income, and called herself a graphics designer as a cover. Easy enough to find out which way the wind blew by running a background check on her.

Well, at least it hadn't required much time or effort to identify the object of Victor Runyon's obsession. If his nemesis, the mysterious telephone caller, was half as simple an ID, I could wash my hands of this whole unpleasant business in a day or so and get on with the routine and impersonal tasks of tracing skips and investigating insurance matters. And the next time Joe DeFalco came sucking around with one of his "favors," I would cheerfully kick his ass out the door.

WHEN I GOT TO MY FLAT in Pacific Heights I called Kerry again, this time at her apartment, and got her machine; she was still working, even though it was getting to be pretty late. After the beep I said, "Hi, babe. It's eight-thirty; I'm home alone and pining away for you. Call me when you get in, if it's not too late. We'll talk dirty to each other."

I ate a light dinner and took to my lonely bed. Read for a while and then turned out the light and lay there hoping the phone would ring before I fell asleep.

It didn't.

Chapter **3**

IN THE MORNING I ran the background check—and a credit check —on Nedra Adams Merchant. She turned out to be thirty-three years of age, divorced, and in fact a fairly prosperous graphics designer who owned and operated Illustrative Image Designs, Inc. Fancy name for a one-woman outfit that specialized in business brochures, convention and sales-promotion posters, and magazine layout. Her business address was different from her home address—a number on Third Street that put it in the SoMa area, within a couple of blocks of the building in which Victor Runyon had his office. That was no surprise. Architect and graphics designer meet somewhere in the area, café or restaurant or maybe one of the showrooms, strike up a conversation, find out they have things in common personally and professionally, one thing leads to another. . . . yeah. Affairs were all so damned cut-and-dried once you got past the emotional baggage and down to the basics. Hell, most things in life were. Emotions are what make the human animal the complex mess he is.

The house at 770 Crestmont had gone to Nedra as part of her divorce settlement five years ago. Her ex-husband, Walter

Merchant, had shared it with her for the five years previous. He was an attorney. It was her first and evidently only marriage and there had been no children.

Her credit rating had been excellent since the divorce—until approximately four months ago. Then, for a period of three months, she had quit paying her bills. Her gas, electricity, and water had all been shut off at the end of July for nonpayment; in early August she'd ponied up the full amounts owed plus penalties and the utilities were now back in service. Last October she'd bought a new Mercedes 540XL, paying one third of the purchase price of more than fifty thousand dollars as a cash down payment. All payments on time until May, then no payments until the first of this month, just in time to forestall a repossession order being issued by her bank.

Again until May, Nedra Merchant had been an active user of half a dozen different credit cards, with a history of prompt payment of the total amount on each card each month. Over the last three and a half months she hadn't used any of the cards even once. Nor had she paid her April Visa, MasterCard, and American Express bills until early August. Again, then, all payments to each company in full.

What all of this seemed to mean was that she'd had some sort of sudden financial crisis in May that had lasted for at least three months and to some extent might still be going on. It would have had to be pretty devastating to wipe out any savings she might have had and to take up so much of her income that she could no longer afford to pay even her utility bills. None of my business what the crisis was unless Victor Runyon was somehow involved. Supporting her since the financial crash? Gave her a lump sum at the end of last month, loan or gift, so she could keep herself afloat? Kay Runyon hadn't mentioned any unaccounted-for expenditures; but it was possible he had cash resources that his wife knew nothing about.

How about Nedra Merchant's ex-husband? Did *he* know anything?

I opened the Yellow Pages to *Attorneys*. Walter Merchant

was listed, with an address on Eucalyptus Drive, under the sub-heading of Personal Injury & Property Damage. He even had a little boxed ad:

Injury Accident Specialist
Quick Settlements
Free Consultation
Medical Care Arranged on Credit
NO WIN—NO FEE

Uh-huh, I thought. I wondered if he was one of the breed of attorney who will take on any case, no matter how ethically marginal, if they see an edge or a loophole or just the bare-bones potential for a fat settlement; the shysters who clog up the court dockets with their money-grubbing briefs, who could not care less if real justice is done, because their only interest in the law is how it can best serve them. More and more of that ilk every year, it seems. Used to be that even the worst of them kept their ambu-lance-chasing out of the public eye, but this is the age of the Big Hype and the Big Buck; what chance do such abstract concepts as professional ethics and integrity stand against rampaging capi-talism? Nowadays the personal-injury boys and girls are all over the media, particularly in saturation TV ads in which they and their "satisfied clients" ballyhoo their dubious accomplishments like pitchmen peddling snake oil. "Joe Smith, *the* dirt bike law-yer, got me $350,000 even though the police report said the accident was my fault and I was charged with felony drunk driv-ing." Was it any wonder there was so much lawyer-bashing these days? Q. How many lawyers does it take to change a light bulb? A. Two. One to stick his finger in the socket and the other to file suit against the electric company.

But attorneys aren't the only breed to take their money-loving ways before the public, up close and personal. Televange-lists started the trend and in some markets are still flourishing; now any number of other professional groups are taking up the advertising cudgel, too, including one I'd have liked to believe was above that kind of hucksterism—the private investigator. Not long ago I'd heard about one licensed P.I., back East somewhere, who had made and marketed a videotape called ''Do You Know Who You're Dating?,'' aimed at people who want to check out potential spouses or housemates before they get too involved. On his video the detective tells you how to identify a philanderer and/or fortune hunter, how to spy on someone, and—naturally— how to go about hiring the ''right kind'' of private investigator.

Maybe one of these nights, I thought, I'll turn on the tube and there Eberhardt will be, wearing one of his cheap suits and Goodwill ties, puffing on a pipe and flogging his services in that stiff, humorless way of his. ''Hello. My name is Eberhardt. I am the sole owner and operator of Eberhardt Investigative Services. My offices are located in a crummy building on Eighteenth and Valencia, but they're only temporary. I specialize in all types of cases and I guarantee results. I do all my own work—I don't need anybody for anything. I'm the best, the smartest, and some-day I'll be the biggest dick in San Francisco.''

But it wasn't funny.

It wasn't funny at all.

EUCALYPTUS DRIVE is on the west side of the city, close to the Stonestown Mall and San Francisco State University. The building in which Walter Merchant did business was a four-story nondescript pile that also housed doctors, dentists, and other professional services. Merchant seemed to be fairly successful at the personal-injury racket: he had a six-room suite on the top floor, and two junior partners. His anteroom wasn't such-a-much: muted colors and a minimum of furniture and decorations, which may or may not have been calculated to provide a businesslike, no-nonsense first impression. Either way, the redheaded legal secretary fit right in. She was young and attractive, but she wore glasses and a severely tailored suit, and her welcoming smile was both courteous and competent.

I gave her one of my business cards and a request to see Walter Merchant on a routine matter concerning his ex-wife. Her only reaction was a slightly raised eyebrow. She invited me to have a seat and took my card through one of the inner doors. I had a seat, and when she didn't return immediately I picked up a copy of *People* magazine and thumbed through it. I was skimming a story about a twenty-five-year-old baseball player who had written a "tell-all" autobiography—ludicrous for several reasons, not the least of which was that a twenty-five-year-old baseball player who could read much less write a book was a Smithsonian rarity—when the secretary reappeared and said that Mr. Merchant was free at the moment and would be happy to give me ten minutes of his time.

Merchant's private office differed from the outer one in that law books covered one wall and a big aquarium stood in front of another. Inside the tank, vividly colored tropical fish darted in and out among rocks and shimmery green underwater plants. "Neons, rasboras, and mollies, mostly," he said when he saw me looking at the tank. "The two yellow-and-white ones with the black-tipped fins are my prizes. Amphiprion percula, very rare." I nodded and smiled, as if I knew or cared what amphiprion percula were. He told me anyway. "Clownfish," he said.

Merchant was more or less what I'd expected. Late thirties, tennis-and-handball trim, with shrewd brown eyes and lank brown hair thinning at the crown. Well but not flashily dressed in a charcoal-gray suit, pale-green shirt, yellow paisley tie; gold watch on one wrist, square opal ring on the third finger of his other hand. Calm, confident, take-charge manner. Vigorous handshake, professional smile. Perry Mason would have been proud of the dignified image he projected.

When we were seated, him behind his exec's desk with his hands tented under his chin in an attentive posture, he said, "I've heard your name, of course. One of our city's foremost investigators."

Me and Hal Lipset, I thought. I showed him a disarming smile of my own and said through it, "I've been at the game a long time." We were like a couple of smart mongrel dogs in an alley, sniffing around each other, trying to pick up the right scent.

"It's not a serious problem that brings you here, I hope."

"Not serious, no."

"Something about my ex-wife."

"A routine insurance matter. I do a fair amount of background checks and claims investigation."

I was prepared to embellish on that with some specific fabrications, but Merchant seemed satisfied. He said, "I see. Well, what is it you'd like to know?"

"You've been divorced five years, is that right?"

"Closer to four and a half."

"Amicable split?"

Small pause. Then he shrugged and settled back in his chair. "Not at the time. There were some bad feelings, wrangling over assets—the usual frictions when two people dissolve a marriage. Once tempers cooled . . . well, she didn't give me any reason to hire a bodyguard and I didn't give her any reason to change the locks on the house."

"So you don't bear her any ill will."

"None whatsoever. Nor does she bear me any."

"Are you on friendly terms?"

"Cordial would be a better word."

"How long since you last saw her?"

"About a year. We had lunch one day last fall."

"Since you talked to her?"

"Six months. I check in with Nedra once or twice a year, to see how she's getting along."

"Do you know much about her current affairs?"

"Affairs? You mean business affairs?"

"Yes."

"Well, I understand she's doing quite well," Merchant said. "Built up her graphics design business into a real money-maker." On that last there was an undercurrent of what might have been resentment, as if he'd have preferred her to be a little less independently successful.

To prod him a little I said, "Not such a money-maker in recent months. She's evidently had severe financial problems—missed utility and credit-card payments and three installments on a new Mercedes before she got caught up again."

"Really?" He seemed genuinely surprised. And a little pleased, too, though he tried not to show it. "That's odd. I mean, I had the exact opposite impression of her finances. That she'd gone to the head of the class."

"How so?"

"My last three alimony checks," Merchant said. "She hasn't cashed them."

My turn to be surprised. "Still hasn't cashed them, you mean?"

"That's right."

"How much are you paying her per month, if you don't mind my asking?"

"Two thousand." Now his smile had a sardonic quirk. "Her design business was struggling when we split up, and she had a good attorney and a sympathetic judge."

"Six thousand dollars total, then."

"Right. Naturally I was delighted. But I thought she was doing me a favor, for old times' sake or out of some latent feeling of guilt. I was planning to call her, as a matter of fact, if she didn't cash the next one. Now . . . well, I don't know what to think."

Neither did I.

I asked, "Why would she have latent feelings of guilt, Mr. Merchant? Something to do with the divorce?"

Another small pause. His manner seemed to shift subtly, to become less guarded, more confidential. "The reason for the divorce," he said.

"Which was?"

"Other men."

"You mean a string of infidelities?"

"Oh yes, a string. The last one in particular."

"I see."

"But it wasn't cheating to her."

"No? What was it then?"

"Adventure, excitement—plot and counterplot. Nedra would have made a good spy. You know, Mata Hari and all that. It's part of her nature."

"Uh-huh."

"I'm not a saint," he said. "What man is? But with Nedra . . . men aren't just a hobby with her. They're an obsession."

That word again.

"And vice versa," Merchant said.

"How do you mean that?"

"Most of her conquests become obsessed with her, sooner or later. That's the kind of woman she is. You'd have to know her to understand exactly what I mean. She gets under the skin of a certain kind of male, and she knows it, and she does everything she can to encourage it."

"Encourage obsession with her?"

"She's a control freak," he said.

"You want to elaborate on that, Mr. Merchant?"

"She gets off on manipulating and dominating men. It gives her a sense of power. Doesn't matter to her whether the men are young or old, blue-collar or white-collar, intelligent or stupid. Or even particularly attractive, God knows."

"Weak men?" I asked, to see what he'd say.

He didn't take offense. He had a thick skin, and probably a healthy dislike for his vulnerability where his ex-wife was concerned; that was part of the reason he was being so candid with me. "To one degree or another," he said, "at least where women are concerned. I fared better than all the rest, though. I got her to marry me, and stay married to me for five years."

"She must have loved you, then."

"As much as Nedra is capable of loving anyone other than herself, yes. Besides, she hadn't really honed her skills in those days."

"You mentioned a man she was seeing before your divorce. Mind telling me who he was?"

"Not at all." Malice in his voice and in his eyes, quick and bright even after five years. "His name is April. Lawrence April."

"And who would Lawrence April be?"

"An investment counselor. Very successful."

"Here in the city?"

"Yes."

"Was Nedra's affair with him a lengthy one?"

"Several months. He begged her to marry him."

"But she said no?"

"She'd had enough of marriage. Dear Nedra."

"How did April take her rejection?"

"He didn't like it. Not in the least."

"Did he make trouble for her?"

"Not for her. For me."

"What kind of trouble?"

"He came to see me. All bent out of shape, half crazy. Blamed me for her turning him down. Said I'd manipulated her, warped her thinking, ruined her for a relationship with a man who really loved her. Meaning himself, of course. Christ, he was totally irrational."

"What happened?"

"I tried to put him out of the house," Merchant said. His mouth twisted at the memory. "He hit me, knocked me down. In my own living room. Broke my cheekbone."

"You have him arrested?"

"No. I thought about it but I decided against it." Another twist of his mouth, this time into a bitterly satisfied smile. "I filed suit against him."

Right, I thought. What else?

"And?"

"It never went to court. I had him by the short hairs and he knew it. On advice of counsel he settled—a very handsome settlement, I might add. It made the divorce quite a bit easier to take."

"Have you had any contact with April since the settlement?"

"No, none."

"I don't suppose Nedra's still seeing him?"

"I'd be amazed if she was."

"The attack on you turn her against him?"

Merchant shook his head. "She never stays with one man too long, particularly the ones who become possessive."

"Can you tell me the names of any of her other lovers?"

"No. Wait, yes, one. Rigsby, I think—Glen Rigsby. I met him once, at one of those coed health clubs downtown. Muscle-bound type. Well-hung, probably. Nedra always did like a sizable prick."

"Customer or employee of this club?"

"Worked there, I believe. I don't remember as what."

"Do you recall the name of the club?"

"Not offhand."

"Located where?"

"SoMa. Not far from Nedra's old office, the one she had before she went upscale."

"Where was that?"

"On Second, near Market."

I nodded. "Let's see . . . I could use the names of one or two of her close woman friends."

"*Close* woman friends? Nedra? As far as I know she doesn't have any. Didn't when we were together. She doesn't like women."

"No?"

"Competition," Merchant said. "The only female she cares about is herself."

"Uh-huh."

"Nedra is the type of woman who sets the feminist movement back fifty years."

I had no comment on that. I got to my feet. "Well, I won't take up any more of your time, Mr. Merchant. Thanks for being so candid with me."

"Not at all." He stood, too, reached for my hand again. While he was pumping it he said, "You're not really investigating an insurance matter."

"I'm not?"

"Routine background checks don't include the kinds of questions you've been asking. It has something to do with Nedra and one of her conquests, doesn't it? Some sort of Sturm und Drang."

I said carefully, "Clients of private detectives have the same privileges as clients of attorneys."

"Of course. I don't care about the details. Call it professional curiosity."

"I can't discuss it in any case."

He shrugged. "I respect that. As I said, I don't really care. I'm over Nedra now. I've been over her for a long time."

The hell he was.

He wouldn't be over Nedra Adams Merchant if he lived to be a hundred and ten.

THOUGHTS WHILE DRIVING DOWNTOWN: So what had I gotten from Walter Merchant? Was his ex-wife the cold-hearted, man-eating bitch he'd portrayed her to be? Or was the portrait a distorted one, painted in colors of bitterness, frustration, vindictive hurt? I'd have liked to believe that the true image of Nedra Adams Merchant was a mixture of good and evil—like the true images of most of us, with shadings toward one extreme or the other. And yet, the things Kay Runyon had told me yesterday, the memory of Victor Runyon entering the Crestmont house with his arms full of flowers, argued in favor of Walter Merchant's representation. Well, I'd have to talk to some other people who knew the lady before I could begin to see her for myself as she really was.

I was inclined to rule out Merchant as the anonymous telephone caller. On the one hand, he was carrying a torch and it might have burned his psyche in bizarre ways. On the other hand, five years is a long time to be still warning men away from an ex-wife; and he obviously enjoyed being the shrewd and successful lawyer, took too much pleasure in *using* the law to get back at his enemies. Threatening phone calls just weren't his style.

The one piece of hard information he'd given me was the uncashed alimony checks. And it made matters even more puzzling. If Nedra Merchant had been in the throes of a financial crisis for three months, why would she fail to make use of six thousand dollars in ready cash?

Chapter 4

LAWRENCE APRIL WAS BLACK.

Merchant hadn't mentioned this fact, which told me something good about Walter Merchant. There was no question that he hated April, but the hatred was strictly personal; it had no racial overtones of any kind. Which made Merchant that embraceable rarity in today's society, a person who was wholly unbigoted, truly color-blind. Shyster lawyer or not, this elevated him several notches in my estimation.

April's offices were downtown on New Montgomery—Cooley and April, Investment Consultants. I figured I would have difficulty getting an audience with him if I used the more or less straightforward approach I had with Merchant, so I went in with a lie ready about being in dire need of financial advice. That wouldn't have gotten me in to see April either; I knew that as soon as I saw the plush decor, the expensive artwork on the walls. This was a high-rolling outfit. Potential clients wearing seventy-five-dollar Ross Dress for Less suits and a tie without a pin or a tack (this morning I'd been unable to find the gold one

Kerry had presented to me last Christmas) would be given the gate as fast as a street person looking for a handout.

The only reason I got to talk to April at all was that he happened to be in the anteroom when I entered, having a discussion with a brittle-looking blond receptionist. As I came up to her desk I heard her call him Mr. April. So I switched gears to the direct approach and said to him, "Excuse me. Are you Lawrence April?"

He looked up. An expression of vague irritation crossed his face when he saw that I wasn't anybody he knew or was likely to want to know. He bore a small resemblance to Harry Belafonte, although his features were more angular and his hair longer than Belafonte had worn it at the same age. Fortyish, lean, with a sensual mouth and hot dark eyes. Self-assured and impeccably dressed in a three-piece Armani suit. He'd have been a good subject for a *Forbes* or *Business Week* profile on the successful black businessman. For all I knew, one had already been done on him.

"Yes?"

"I wonder if I might have a few minutes of your time."

"I'm afraid not. I have a full schedule today. If you'll state your business to Ms. Green, perhaps she—"

"It's a private matter," I said.

"Oh?"

"Concerning Nedra Adams Merchant."

It was as if I'd driven a bolt through his neck and down the length of his spine; his body reacted with the same seizurelike stiffening. His eyes seemed to ignite, then to glow like drops of molten glass. A man prone to sudden rages, for a fact. You could see the turbulence working in him, the struggle for control of it that was going on at the same time.

He said, "Who are you?" in a dead-cold voice.

I handed him one of my cards. He read it, looked at me again with something close to hatred. Then he put the card in his pocket and said to the receptionist, "If you'll just make that call, Andrea." To me he said, "Five minutes, no more," and turned on his heel and went through a door and along a hallway beyond. I trailed after him.

His private office was considerably more opulent than Walter Merchant's, complete with a small mahogany wet bar. The carpet and the upholstered chairs were an elegant silver-gray. On one wall I noted a framed diploma that said he had an M.B.A. from Stanford. On his desk, angled so that I had a clear look at it from where I stood, was a gold-framed photograph of an attractive African-American woman and two male preteens.

April didn't invite me to sit down; he didn't sit down himself. As soon as he shut the door he moved in on me until his nose was about six inches from mine. I don't like my space invaded, particularly in an aggressive fashion, but I let him get away with it. I was not about to give ground and I didn't want to make the situation any more unpleasant by crowding *him.*

He said between his teeth, "Who sent you here?"

"Nobody sent me, Mr. April. I—"

"Five years. It's been five years."

"What has?"

Veins pulsed on his temples, on his eyelids. "What do you want?"

"To ask you a few questions about Nedra Merchant."

"What kind of questions?"

"Pertaining to a matter I'm investigating—"

"What matter? Whom are you investigating?"

"Not you, Mr. April."

"Nedra?"

"Among others."

"If you try to drag my name into any sort of scandal . . ."

"I don't do divorce work, Mr. April, if that's what you mean. I'm a reputable investigator and have been for more than twenty-five years. If you doubt that, I'll give you half a dozen references and you can check them out before you say another word to me. Fair enough?"

His eyes remained fixed on mine, but the heat in them was cooling. His face lost some of its blood-swell. After ten seconds or so, he abruptly backed off and ran a long-fingered hand over his face.

"I suppose," he said, and stopped, and then went on with it, "I suppose you know all the sordid details of my relationship with Nedra."

"I'm not interested in sordid details, Mr. April."

"But you do know all about it."

"I've been told some things."

"She was the biggest mistake of my life," he said. "I don't like to be reminded of it. You can understand that, can't you?"

"Yes, I can. If you'll just answer some nonthreatening questions, I'll go away and you can forget about her again. About me too."

He moved away from me, to the wall where the framed diploma hung. He appeared to stare at it for about thirty seconds, but I doubted that he was actually seeing it. Then he turned and came back to face me again, not too close this time.

"What is it you want to know?"

"To begin with, how long it's been since you've seen or talked to Nedra Merchant."

"Nearly five years. When I came to my senses after the incident with that shyster husband of hers . . . you know about that?"

"Yes."

"In explicit detail, no doubt, if you've spoken to him. As I expect you have." When I didn't respond to that he said, "All right. Once I accepted the fact that I'd made an utter fool of myself over Nedra Merchant, I vowed never to have anything to do with her again. For my sake, for the sake of my family, and for the sake of my business partner and clients."

"And you haven't broken that vow."

"I have not."

"Have you kept tabs on her, on her career?"

"No."

"Don't have any idea how her graphics design business is doing."

"No."

"Suppose I told you she's had serious financial problems in recent months."

"I'd tell you I'm sorry to hear it, the same as I'd be sorry to hear anyone is in financial difficulty."

"What if she came to you for advice? Or a loan?"

"She didn't."

"It was a hypothetical question."

"I would refuse to see her. Under no circumstances would I offer my professional services to Nedra or loan her so much as a penny."

I nodded. "Were there other men in her life while you were seeing her?"

"Her ex-husband."

"Other than him."

"No."

"You're certain of that?"

"I would have known," he said.

"But you weren't her first extramarital affair."

"No. She admitted that to me. But she was forced into accepting the attentions of other men."

"Forced by who? Walter Merchant?"

"His stifling treatment of her, yes. It wasn't something she was proud of. Why do you suppose she was seeing a therapist?"

"I didn't know she was seeing a therapist."

"For some time before I met her."

"Man or woman?"

"Man."

"Do you recall his name?"

"Duncan? Something like that."

"Offices downtown here?"

"I don't remember where his offices were."

"Did she feel he was helping her?"

"She seemed to. In my opinion he was a crutch."

"You're not a believer in long-term therapy?"

"No."

"Did she ever talk to you about her former lovers?"

"Hardly."

"Never let even one name slip?"

"No."

"And you didn't ask?"

"I didn't want to know."

"So you wouldn't have any idea who she's been involved with since the end of your affair."

"No. Nor do I care."

"Do you know a health club employee named Glen Rigsby?"

"No."

"How about an architect, Victor Runyon?"

"No."

The names didn't seem to sting him any, as they might have if he, like Merchant, was carrying a torch. That strengthened my impression that he'd been telling me the truth.

I asked, "How long did your affair last?"

"A little over four months."

"You must have gotten to know her fairly well in that length of time." The look on his face made me add, "Or did you?"

"Not as well as I thought I knew her," April said. "What kind of food and music and shows she liked, what gave her pleasure, what made her laugh and cry. But not what she was like down deep inside."

"The real Nedra Merchant."

"Yes. Glimpses, that was all. Just . . . glimpses."

"How would you characterize her?"

"As a good person, basically. Kind, generous."

"Caring, loving?"

"To a point."

"What point is that?"

"The point when things . . . when I allowed matters to get completely out of hand. When I told her I was ready to throw away my marriage and my family for her. Then she rebelled."

"Rebelled?"

"She became cold, distant. Possessiveness turned her off, she said. She'd had enough of that from her husband. Once she was free of him, she wouldn't permit herself to be tied down again to anyone."

"So she's the one who ended your relationship."

"Yes. I was bitter at the time, but now I understand that she had my best interests at heart, as well as her own. Forcing me out of her life was an act of kindness."

"Then you don't think it would have worked for the two of you in the long run."

"No. Not anymore I don't."

"Why not?"

"Many reasons. Race, temperament, attitude, the fact that I really didn't know her and she didn't know me. What we had . . . it was physical, not spiritual."

"One person I talked to thinks she's obsessed with men. That she's a control freak who uses them for her own amusement, then casts them aside. Would you say there's any truth in that?"

April frowned. "No, I wouldn't. She isn't that way."

"Isn't a controlling personality? Doesn't encourage her lovers to become obsessed with her?"

"Absolutely not."

"But *you* were obsessed with her."

"The fault was mine, not hers. I suppose the person who defamed her character is Walter Merchant?"

I neither confirmed nor denied it.

"Have you met Nedra? Talked to her at any length?"

"No," I said, "not yet."

"When you do," April said, "you'll see the truth. She's not some sort of modern-day Circe, for God's sake. She is a good, warm person who . . ." He couldn't seem to find the rest of what he wanted to say. He finished lamely, or maybe not so lamely, "She's innocent."

Maybe he believed that, but I didn't. She might not be the wicked sorceress of Walter Merchant's depiction; she might even be the basically good person who lived in Lawrence April's memory. But whatever Nedra Adams Merchant really was, she damned well wasn't innocent.

THERE ARE HALF A DOZEN health and athletic clubs in the SoMa area, where you can swim, play tennis and racquet ball, take aerobic and tae kwon do classes, work on the old jump shot, lift weights, challenge Nautilus machines, and sweat your ass off —literally—in steam rooms. Two of them hadn't been there five years ago; two others were out in the Showplace Square area, a couple of miles west. The remaining two were within walking distance of New Montgomery, and of Nedra Merchant's old office on Second Street, and it took me a little better than an hour to check out the pair of them.

Nobody at either place knew Nedra Adams Merchant.

Nobody at either place had ever heard of a man named Glen Rigsby.

WHEN I GOT BACK to my office I found one message waiting. From Kay Runyon: Had I found out anything yet? Would I please call her as soon as possible?

No, I would not please call as soon as possible. I was not ready yet to make a report; I wanted a better handle on Nedra Merchant first. Premature reports do more harm than good. All too often they distort the facts and build more anxiety than they relieve. A prime example of that is the broadcast media's handling of sudden-disaster situations, such as the '89 earthquake. They disseminate all sorts of conflicting and hyperbolic information, whip everybody into a frenzy, and then after it's all over, instead of issuing apologies they blithely pat themselves on the back with endless promos telling you what a fine job of "responsible reporting" they did.

Another thing Kay Runyon wanted was her hand held. I didn't blame her for that, but I'm no good at coddling and empty reassurances. It's awkward for me and awkward for the client.

I looked up Glen Rigsby in the White Pages. No listing

under that name, nor under G. Rigsby. I tried a few variants in case Walter Merchant had misremembered the exact name: Rigby, Grigsby, Grigby. No listing under any of those either.

So maybe he lived in another Bay Area city. Or maybe he'd moved to Blue Ball, Pennsylvania, or maybe he was dead: five years is a long time. And even if I did find him alive and cooperative, he was a prohibitive long shot to be the threatening caller.

I checked in the White Pages, then in the Yellow Pages under *Physicians—Psychiatry* and under *Psychologists.* Nobody named Duncan was listed. It might be that Lawrence April had misremembered *his* name. Or he worked for a clinic. Or he had moved away, or changed professions, or retired, or died. And if I found *him* alive and still practicing, professional ethics would prevent him from telling me anything revealing about Nedra Merchant. Besides which, a psychiatrist or psychologist was a highly unlikely candidate for a phone freak.

Not for the first time today I thought: What the hell am I doing all this for? Chances are, it's going to break open by itself before much longer. If Nedra Merchant was in fact a man-eater, she was due to toss Victor Runyon over pretty soon anyway, for the crime of possessiveness. When that happened, the caller would go away, too, to devil Nedra's next conquest. Kay Runyon confronting her wasn't likely to do either of them any good, and it was not going to save the marriage; if their little family unit was to be saved at all, it would be by Victor coming to his senses as Lawrence April had apparently done.

Just a job, another job—sure. Do your work, earn some money to pay the bills. But the work ought to matter, right? Or at least you ought to be able to convince yourself that it matters while you're doing it, even if you suspect in your more cynical moments that it doesn't mean much in the long run and that maybe not a hell of a lot of human endeavor does. I had never been somebody who could just go through the motions. And that was what this felt like—going through the motions, for no real purpose, to no real resolution.

Well, then? Nobody to blame but myself. Mr. Bleeding

Heart. Seduced by a sob story in a Dreamsicle room by a woman who paints pictures with dryer lint. It made me feel like the butt of some cruel cosmic joke. Mr. Bleeding Heart? Mr. Butthead.

I called TRW and requested a credit check on Glen Rigsby or Grigsby, picking the two most likely spellings. While I was at it I asked for credit checks on Lawrence April and Walter Merchant as well. Then I called the AMA and the San Francisco Bay Area Psychological Association, and requested information on a psychiatrist/psychologist/therapist named Duncan practicing in San Francisco five years ago. Might as well give Kay Runyon full value for the fifty-five dollars an hour she was paying me.

I had paperwork to do, and preliminaries on a department-store skip trace that could be done telephonically, but I didn't feel like knuckling down to any of it. Grumpy and out of sorts today. It wasn't just the Runyon case either. It was spending too damn much time inside my own head lately. Work all day, sit around my flat at night. Some boring company Mr. Butthead was.

I needed to get laid.

No, that was more cynicism. I needed Kerry—not just her body, *her.* Her smile, her wit, her fussiness, her insight, her caring, her friendship. Kerry Wade, soulmate. Sounded trite and a little silly, when you put it that way, but it was true. I was a loner, without many friends; had been one most of my life. And since Eberhardt had walked out, I seemed to want even less to do with the few friends I had left. Afraid to get too close to them, afraid to trust them too much, for fear of being hurt again: Eberhardt's goddamn legacy. So now even more than ever I'd put all my faith and social eggs in Kerry's basket, and damn it, I *missed* her—

The telephone rang.

And it was Kerry.

I grinned when I heard her voice. Psychic connection, by God. Didn't this prove that we were soulmates?

"I got home too late to call you last night," she said. "Yesterday was total crap. Today's not much better so far."

"You sound pretty tired." Preoccupied too.

"Frazzled is the word. I would have called this morning if I'd had two minutes to myself."

"I figured you were busy."

"Three different accounts, all wanting instant results," she said. "Bridger's the worst. Bridger is driving me up a wall."

"Who he?"

"Granny's Bakeries. He's Granny. He's also a jerk. If he calls one more time—" She broke off; I heard her take a ragged breath. "You don't want to hear all this, not during business hours. You must be busy too."

"Not at the moment."

"You okay? I mean, getting enough sleep?"

"I'd sleep better if I had company."

Nothing from her.

"Hey, I'm not complaining," I said. "And I do want to hear about it."

"Hear about what?"

"All your troubles with Granny Bridger and the rest. How about tonight?"

"I can't tonight. I've got a pro-choice meeting after I get done here."

"Tomorrow night, then."

"Not tomorrow either."

"The weekend? You're not going to work all weekend again?"

"I don't know," she said. "I may have to."

"Kerry, baby, I miss you. I haven't seen you in more than a week—"

"I know that—"

"I *miss* you."

"I miss you too. But I don't know if—" She broke off again, this time because a woman's voice in the background called her name, said that Paul somebody was waiting to see her.

There was a muffled rattle of conversation; then Kerry said to me, sounding even more frazzled and preoccupied, "I've got to go. Another emergency."

"Try to free up Saturday or Sunday night, okay?"

"I'll call you," she said, and rang off.

Chapter **5**

IT MUST HAVE BEEN a slow day at TRW: one of the reps called back after only forty-five minutes with the information I'd requested. The credit reports on Lawrence April and Walter Merchant told me nothing much; both had excellent ratings and a long history of paying their various bills on time. The one piece of potentially useful news concerned a man named Glenford Grigsby, who lived in Oakland and who was currently employed by an outfit called Health House in Emeryville.

Grigsby's credit rating wasn't so hot. Neither was his past employment record. He'd worked for nine different health and athletic clubs over the past fifteen years, as a masseur, a gym attendant, and an "exercise therapist," whatever that was. One of the clubs he'd worked for, five years ago, was a SoMa establishment called The New You that had been located on Hawthorne Street within easy walking distance of Nedra Merchant's former office. I hadn't visited The New You yesterday because it wasn't there anymore; it had gone out of business in 1989.

After the TRW rep and I were done with each other, I got Health House's number from directory assistance and called it and asked the man who answered if Glenford Grigsby was working today. Affirmative. It was a quarter to three by my watch; the Bay Bridge wouldn't be too crowded yet with homeward-bound commuters. If I hustled I could still get over to Emeryville, talk to Grigsby, and get back into the city before the big rush got under way.

HEALTH HOUSE WAS A SPRAWLING, newish complex on the bay side of Highway 80, with easy access to the freeway. Designed for busy office workers, guests of nearby hotels, and residents of the condo high-rises in the area. It had just about anything you could want in the way of healthful pursuits, from indoor tennis courts and swimming pool on down to aerobics classes. Grigsby, according to a woman at the front desk, was something of a jack-of-all-trades, working wherever he was needed within the complex. She consulted a chart and said that right now he was providing competition for one of the members on the handball courts. I told her I had important business with him, and she decided I looked respectable enough to be given a pass into the bowels of the place.

The handball courts were on the ground floor, rear. There were three of them but only one was in use. One of the players was middle-aged, wiry, and intense; he attacked the ball as if it were an enemy he was trying to hurt. The other player was in his thirties, blond, muscled, the Adonis type—Grigsby, from Walter Merchant's description. He played with a fluid grace, hard enough to work up a good sweat, but I got the impression he was holding back, letting the older man have the advantage. Good employee, deferring to a member . . . or maybe he just didn't give a damn about winning a contest in which there was nothing for him but a workout.

I was there ten minutes before the match ended, in a volley so furious the ball caroming off the walls and ceiling was a blur. The older guy won, but he was so drained from the effort he had to lean against the wall to shake hands. Both men used towels and had swigs from plastic water bottles; then they said some things to each other, and the blonde laughed and clapped the wiry one on the back. The older man came out first and walked away stiffly toward the men's locker room. The Adonis gathered up ball and gloves and towels and water bottles before he quit the court.

"Are you Glen Grigsby?"

He stopped, gave me a neutral look, and said, "That's me. I hope you don't want to play handball. Pretty fast in there just now. I'm pooped."

"No handball. It's information I'm after, not exercise."

"That so? What kind of information?"

"About Nedra Merchant."

The name didn't seem to have much of an effect on him, except to make him look at me in a different way: mildly interested, faintly amused. "What are you, another member of the club?"

"What club is that?"

"The Hard-on for Nedra Society," Grigsby said, and laughed.

"If I were," I said, "I might take offense at that."

He shrugged. "Why bother me, friend? I haven't seen Nedra in two or three years."

"No contact with her of any kind?"

"Sexual or otherwise," he said. "Listen, nice talking to you, but I've got to get a shower before I chill. Give Nedra my love."

He moved off at a fast walk. I trailed after him, into the men's locker room where the older handball player had stripped down and was padding naked into the showers. Grigsby opened a locker, frowned when he saw me standing a few feet away.

"Something else?" he said.

"More questions. If you don't mind."

"Told you, I've got to get a shower."

"I can wait."

"Look, friend," he said, hard, and then seemed to think better of what he was about to say. A wariness crept into his expression. He didn't know who I was or what I wanted and he didn't want to push me if I was somebody who could do him harm. Maybe he was afraid of losing another job. "Tell me what this is all about, then maybe we can talk. You're not a cop?"

"What do you think?"

"I think you'd better show me your badge if you are."

I showed him the Photostat of my investigator's license. It didn't impress him, but he didn't sneer at it either. He was still wary.

"Like I said, friend, I haven't seen Nedra in a long time. You can't drag me into anything connected with her."

"Such as what?"

"Such as anything. We had our fling, she went her way and I went mine. And that's the name of that tune."

"How long did your fling last?"

"Six weeks, give or take."

"Not very long."

"Long enough."

"For what?"

"For me to say sayonara."

"So you're the one who broke it off?"

"I'm the one. That's the way I prefer it."

"Why? I mean, why did you end it with Nedra?"

"I figured out what she wanted, that's why."

"And what was that?"

"Not my hot bod," Grigsby said. "Sex wasn't enough for her. Not little Nedra."

"No?"

"No. She wanted somebody to kiss her feet as well as her ass, you know what I mean?"

"Not exactly."

"Worshipers, that's the kind Nedra goes for. Guys who fall all over themselves when she's around, treat her like a goddess, give up everything for her. She picked wrong when she picked me. I don't get on my knees for any woman, not outside the bedroom."

"How did she take it when you walked? Upset, was she?"

"Nah," Grigsby said. "Philosophical. Lots of fish in the sea, that's her attitude."

"That was five years ago?"

"More like six."

"So she was still married at the time."

"Married but thinking about getting unmarried, the way she talked. I don't mess with women with rings on their fingers, not usually, but she came on so strong, and she's such a sweet piece . . . well, hell, you know how it is."

"Yeah, I know how it is."

"Figured you did." He'd put the handball equipment in the locker and now he was stripping off his sweats. "Shower time," he said. Then he said, "No peeking now," and gave me a grin that I didn't return as he skinned out of his jockstrap. He took himself off to the showers.

I stayed put. The older guy came back and slid a curious glance my way, but he didn't say anything. He was dressed in a suit and tie by the time Grigsby came back.

"Christ, you still here?"

"I'm still here."

"Now what do you want to know?" He began working on his muscle-and-sinew with a towel, vigorously.

"Six years since you broke it off with Nedra," I said, "but you told me it's only been two or three since the last time you saw her."

"That's right. But I didn't start up with her again, if that's what's in your head. I ran into her one night in Jack London Square. Hell, she looked right through me. Couldn't be bothered saying hello to a nobody, even if the nobody did make her come twenty or thirty times, once."

"Why do you say it like that, the nobody reference?"

"Guy she was with is somebody."

"Public figure?"

"In your town, yeah."

"Name him."

His mouth got sly. "Cost you twenty bucks."

I took a ten out of my wallet and waggled it in front of his nose. "This is all it's worth to me."

"I'll take it," Grigsby said, and grinned, and made the ten disappear inside his locker. "What the hell, I'd have given you the name for nothing."

"I'm waiting."

"Dean Purchase," he said.

". . . That better be straight, and no mistake."

"It's straight, no mistake."

Dean Purchase. Well, well.

Purchase was a VIP on the San Francisco political scene: one-time assistant director of public works; former supervisor, with two terms on the board in the late seventies and early eighties; special adviser to two previous mayors and chief administrative assistant to the present one. Old San Francisco money; his family had been in city banking since the days of Charles Crocker. He was brash, boisterous, arrogant, and a publicity hound. He was also married to a local socialite and had half a dozen children.

Dean Purchase and Nedra Adams Merchant. An interesting combination, if true. Based on his public persona, Purchase didn't seem to be the kind of man who would fall under the spell of an alleged control freak. But there was no telling what he was like underneath, where women were concerned. Or just how manipulating and persuasive Nedra could be when she wanted a man. Purchase may have represented a major challenge to her: a public figure, a man in a position of power. If power was in fact her bag, sexually controlling a powerful man, even for a little while, would be a consummate thrill.

But even if that were true, was a Purchase-Nedra liaison relevant to my investigation? Glen Grigsby was the type who might stoop to anonymous threatening telephone calls, but Purchase wasn't. If he wanted to hurt you, he'd go right ahead and do it in the open, no pussyfooting around. He might have had a fling with Nedra, she might even have got deep under his skin for a while, but I couldn't see him doing anything in the long run to jeopardize his career and family standing, not for her or for any other woman. He used people, people didn't use him.

Talk to Purchase about Nedra or not? Hard choice. If I opened up a can of worms he'd welded shut, he could do me some damage; he had enough clout if he felt like using it. Chances were, he'd be a dead-end and a waste of time anyway. Better to just let it go and concentrate my efforts in areas that were more likely to be productive. Right?

Right.

So I drove back across the Bay Bridge and took the Fell-Laguna exit and went straight to city hall.

PURCHASE HAD A LARGE private office just down the corridor from the mayor's, and not one but two secretaries on duty in the anteroom. He was in a meeting, I was told, and besides which, his schedule was such that he never saw anyone—not *anyone,* sir—without an appointment. Perhaps if I left my name and the nature of my business, he would be willing to grant me one. . . .

I asked for an envelope, wrote Purchase's name and the word "Personal" on the front. Then, on one of my business cards, I wrote: "Regarding Nedra Merchant. Matter not pertaining directly to you, strictly confidential." I underlined confidential three times, added my signature, sealed the card inside the envelope, and left it with the secretaries.

A mistake, maybe. But I get stubborn—and nowadays, a little reckless—when I'm trying to open a tough nut. I also don't like to be intimidated, especially by a man who doesn't even know I exist.

Chapter **6**

VICTOR RUNYON WAS BACK at 770 Crestmont that evening.

And this time he wasn't alone.

I drove up there because I had nowhere else to go, nothing else to do. A long, solitary evening in my flat was definitely out; I didn't feel like a show or any of the city's other nighttime attractions. I hung around the office until after six-thirty, finishing up the paperwork. Then, when the rest of the building's tenants went home and the night silence closed down, I locked up and got my car and headed for Forest Hill.

They were out in front of Nedra Merchant's red-shingled house, Runyon and a husky, balding man in workman's garb. The gate in the redwood fence was open and Runyon stood in the opening, as if blocking access; the other man faced him in a flat-footed, belligerent stance. They were arguing about something. Heatedly. I drove by, turned at the dead-end circle, and came back. Runyon's BMW was parked behind an off-white Ford Econoline van; I veered to a stop in front of the van, shut off the engine. Good vantage point: I was less than thirty yards away.

The two of them were still arguing. I had my window down

but I couldn't make out what they were saying; the wind was stronger up here tonight and noisy in the high tension wires and the woods above and below. The balding man was becoming more and more agitated, waving his arms to emphasize what he was saying, his nose about three inches from Runyon's. Runyon stood his ground, shaking his head in a helpless kind of way.

This is going to get ugly, I thought. I put my hand on the door release—and in that instant it got ugly.

The balding guy shoved Runyon without warning, a two-handed blow to the chest that slammed him hard into the gate. Runyon bounced back at him like a ball rebounding, his hands coming up in front of his face. He didn't want to fight; the movement of his hands was defensive. The other man didn't read it that way, or didn't want to read it that way. He hit Victor Runyon in the face, closed fist this time, and knocked him backward and down inside the fence. Then he went charging in after him, out of my sight.

I was free of the car by then, but it took me a few seconds to run between it and the van and then across the street and through the gate. Christ! Runyon was still down, on his back moaning, the balding guy straddling him and punching him with both hands in a kind of frenzy. There was blood all over Runyon's face, flecks of it flying from a smashed nose to splatter the red-wood decking around his head.

I caught the balding guy's shoulder, jerked backward. No good. He was ox-strong and half crazed; he shrugged me off and kept right on hitting Runyon, making a series of snorting sounds like an animal in a rut. To get him loose I had to go to one knee, wrap an arm around his neck and then heave and twist him backward, over on his side. As soon as I did that he started fighting me, or trying to. He couldn't do any damage because I was bigger, heavier, and had enough leverage to keep most of his body pinned under mine.

The one eye I could see was glazed and rolling at first, like a blue marble under a film of plastic; then it regained focus, and some of the straining wildness went out of him. He said in a choked voice, "Goddamn you, let me go."

"Not until you cool down."

"I'll break your fuggin head."

"You think so? Maybe I'll break yours instead."

The one eye glared at me for three or four seconds. Then the heat in it died, all at once like a light going off, and he went limp under me. "All right," he said with his mouth against the deck. "All right. All right."

I held on to him awhile longer, to make sure he had his wits back and wasn't going to give me any more trouble. He did and he wasn't; he stayed limp when I finally eased my grip. I shoved off him, up onto my feet, and backpedaled a couple of paces. Victor Runyon was still sprawled on his back, still moaning; his face was lacerated in half a dozen places, his nose bent toward his right cheekbone. Spiderwebs of blood covered the lower half of his face, the fronts of his blue shirt and blue sport jacket.

"Proud of yourself?" I asked the balding guy.

"He had it coming." The words were muffled; on one knee now, he was sucking the bruised and torn knuckles of his right hand.

"You might have killed him."

"Might of had that coming too."

"Is that right? Why? Who are you?"

"Who the hell are *you,* slick?"

"A friend of Runyon's."

"Yeah? Or Nedra's, huh? Another of hers."

"Her what? Boyfriends? Is that what you are?"

"Asshole," he said.

Neither of us had anything for the other; we were just wasting breath. I watched him get slowly to his feet. He was one of those people whose age is difficult to gauge: he might have been anywhere from twenty-five to forty. He had a blocky, ridged face, but with skin that was red as a radish and baby-smooth except for pale, downy brows—as if some curious chemistry had produced an infant that resembled a fully grown adult male.

What was left of his hair was tobacco-colored and as thin and wispy as a dust mouse.

He said, "Hell with it. For now," and swung away abruptly through the gate.

I went after him. There was nobody else out there, nobody visible at any of the neighboring houses. It seemed as though the three of us had made a lot of noise, but it always does when you're in the midst of something violent. The wind was an effective muffler, too, this high on a hillside. Even if any of the neighbors had been alerted, I thought, they probably wouldn't do anything about it. Hear no evil, see no evil.

The balding man was halfway across the street. I called, "Maybe I ought to notify the cops," to see what his reaction would be.

Not much. "Go ahead," he said without slowing or turning.

"Aggravated assault. That's a felony."

No response.

"So is making threatening telephone calls."

Another bust. He was at the van now; he yanked open the door, hauled himself inside. The engine revved, the gears ground, and he came away from the curb in a fast, tight U-turn, the van's front bumper scraping the front bumper of my car. There was not enough room for him to complete the turn in the street; he bounced his wheels up onto the sidewalk, forcing me to jump back out of the way. With one hand he got the van straightened, with the other he gave me the finger. Five seconds later he was gone around the uphill turn.

Hell with it. For now.

Yeah. For now. But I'd see him again—soon.

I have good vision, and there was still plenty of daylight on the street: I'd gotten the van's license number before he'd made me jump.

I wrote the number down in my notebook: insurance against forgetting it or misremembering or transposing any of the letters or numerals. When I came back through the gate I saw that Victor Runyon had raised himself into a sitting position; but his eyes had a painglaze on them and it was obvious that he still wasn't tracking very well. I moved past him to the front door, tried the latch. Locked. I pushed the bell, kept my finger on it for about ten seconds. No answer. If Nedra Merchant was in there, she wasn't dealing with any of this little drama.

Runyon was trying to get to his feet. I helped him, with one arm around his waist for support. "Let me have your key, Mr. Runyon."

"Key?" he said.

"To the house. So we can go inside."

It didn't seem to register. So I patted his jacket pockets, found his keycase and fished it out; he didn't seem to know what I was doing. I walked him to the door, tried two keys before I located one that unlocked it, and took him inside.

Hallway. Closed door to the garage on the left, staircase to the lower floor on the right; beyond the staircase, a smallish formal living room opened at the front, dappled now with sunlight. At the rear on that side, a dining room. Kitchen straight ahead. Another room—probably a family room—was closed off from the hall and from the kitchen by sliding panel doors.

Silence.

A faint musty odor, as if the place had been closed up a long time. Or not cleaned in a long time.

I took Runyon into the sunlit kitchen. Fine ocean view from here, and a wide balcony across the entire rear width of the house so that you could sit outside on nice days to enjoy it. I got Runyon into one of the two chairs at a dinette table. Found a dishtowel under the sink and ran water over it and then used it to sponge some of the blood off his face. He winced and mewled a little when I touched his broken nose. Otherwise he just sat there, neither helping nor hindering me.

Cut on his upper lip, cut on one cheek, neither one deep or long enough to require stitches. Some bruises and abrasions. The only real damage was to his nose, the source of most of the blood. He'd be all right. Physically, at least.

I opened the refrigerator, looking for ice. There was nothing in it. Nothing in the freezer compartment, nothing in the regular compartment—as bare as if it had just been delivered by Sears.

What the hell?

I rinsed out the bloody towel in cold water, took it to Runyon. He looked up at me blankly, like a child. "For your nose," I said, and he nodded and held the towel against his face.

There was an uneasy feeling inside me now. I went into the hallway, opened the door to the garage. Empty. I shut the door, started for the stairs, changed my mind and walked over and opened the sliding door to the closed-off room adjacent to the kitchen.

It was like entering a church. Or a funeral parlor.

Two layers of drapes were closed against the lowering sun; the room—family room, as I'd guessed—was full of dark-light and shadows, the shadows given a grotesque, shimmery animation by the unstable glow from a pair of burning candles. So Runyon hadn't just arrived when the balding guy showed up and braced him; he'd been here awhile, in this room. The candles were on a heavy marble-topped coffee table, flanking something oddly shaped that I couldn't identify from the doorway. Something that contained a lot of flowers: the damp, sweet smell of them was cloying in the airless space.

Carefully, with the little hairs prickling on my neck, I crossed the darkened room. Two candles, tall and black, in sculpted silver holders. The odd-shaped arrangement between them was a kind of bower: red and yellow roses, carnations, three or four other varieties—the bouquets Runyon had bought last night, all of them recently sprayed with water to keep them fresh. And in the midst of the flowers, an eight-by-ten photograph of a woman in an expensive silver frame. I leaned down to it. Dark, slender woman in some kind of Asian outfit, although she herself didn't appear to be Asian; waist-length dark hair, sultry smile. Across the front, in a bold hand, was written: *To darling Vic. My love, Nedra.*

A shrine.

That was the only word for what I was looking at here—a queer, homemade shrine.

I took myself out of there, stumbling once on the carpet in my haste. Runyon hadn't moved from the dinette table; his eyes were closed, the wet towel tight against his nose and turning crimson again. I gripped his shoulder, shook him gently. Shook him again, harder, until his eyes snapped open and lifted to meet mine. They were focused now; he was more or less aware of externals.

"Where's Nedra?" I asked him.

His head wagged brokenly.

"Vic, where's Nedra Merchant?"

". . . Gone," he said.

"Gone? Gone where?"

"Gone," he said again. His features seemed to crumple like old paper, and he laid his head on his arms and began to weep.

I MADE A QUICK, superficial search of the rest of the house. Downstairs was a master bedroom, a spare bedroom, an office, two baths, a small storage area—and nothing out of the ordinary in any of them. Nedra Merchant's bedroom had its own private black-tiled bath and was done in an exotic Oriental style—or what an Occidental might perceive to be an exotic Oriental style. Black teak furniture, ornamental masks and jade statuettes, gold drapes and carpeting and counterpane on the big, round bed. And mirrors, lots of ornate-framed mirrors strategically placed so that Nedra and her bed partners could watch themselves at play.

Man-eater, maybe. Sybarite, probably.

Gone, definitely.

And yet, most if not all of her clothes were still here. The walk-in closet was jammed with casual and evening wear; her dresser drawers were loaded with lingerie; her jewelry case was full of earrings and bracelets and the like, accent on jade items that had to be reasonably expensive; and I'd noticed a matching set of Gucci luggage out in the storage room. All her cosmetics and perfumes appeared to be here, too, neatly arranged on the vanity table in the bath.

Some sort of extended vacation or business trip?

Planned disappearance, for personal reasons or financial gain?

Foul play?

Whatever it was, and however long she'd been gone, Victor Runyon had continued coming here two and three times a week ever since. Why? In the hope that she'd come back? To try to find a clue to her whereabouts? Or to keep renewing his sick little shrine with fresh flowers and fresh candles—an ongoing vigil, votive offerings to God or the gods asking her safe return, a continual private wake? Jesus. The man was not simply obsessed with Nedra Adams Merchant; he was coming apart at the seams, walking the edge of nightmare.

On the table next to Nedra Merchant's bed was a black-and-gold telephone. I picked up the receiver, heard a dial tone, then tapped out Runyon's home number from my notebook. Two rings, and Kay Runyon's voice said a guarded hello.

I identified myself. "We need to talk, Mrs. Runyon."

"You've found out who Nedra is?"

"Yes, but it's more than that. A whole lot more."

". . . Do you want to come here? Vic's . . . away again tonight."

"I know. I'm with him now. There's been some trouble."

Faint intake of breath. "Trouble?"

"He's been hurt. Not too badly, but he needs medical attention. I'm going to take him to the emergency room at S.F. General. Will you meet me there in half an hour?"

"My God, what happened?"

"He was attacked. I'll tell you about it when I see you. Half an hour at S.F. General."

"Yes," she said, "yes, I'll be there."

I went back upstairs, into the kitchen. Runyon wasn't there. Family room, I thought—and that was where he was, sitting now on a long sofa in front of his shrine, staring fixedly at Nedra

Merchant's photograph. The dancing candlelight made his bruised and bloodied face look ghastly, as if he'd been made up for some sort of horror show.

I said, "Time to go, Mr. Runyon."

"Go? Go where?"

"The hospital. Get that broken nose taken care of."

"I don't want to go to the hospital."

"It hurts now but it'll hurt a hell of a lot more if you don't have it set pretty soon."

"I can live with pain," he said. "I've lived with pain a long time now."

"Not the broken-nose kind. On your feet, Mr. Runyon."

He didn't give me any argument. He stood, slowly, took one last lingering look at the photo, and then shambled out of there. He didn't think to snuff the candles; I had to do it for him.

When I joined him in the foyer he gave me a clear-eyed look for the first time. "I don't know you," he said.

"That's right, you don't."

"What are you doing here? Why did you help me?"

I was not about to coddle or play games with him. I said, "I'm a private investigator. Your wife hired me to find out about Nedra."

". . . A detective? Kay?"

"Did you think she didn't know?"

"Poor Kay," he said.

"Yeah. Poor Kay."

"I didn't want to hurt her. I never wanted to hurt my family."

Caught, trapped, backed up against their own deceit, people always say things like that. But the words are hollow; not lies so much as empty afterthoughts. "If you didn't want to hurt your family, you should have stayed away from Nedra Merchant."

"I couldn't."

They say that too. And the next:

"I love her. You don't know how much I love her."

"I don't care how much you love her. Where is she?"

"Gone."

"You said that before. Gone where?"

"I don't know."

"Gone when, then? How long?"

"May. Early May."

"Of her own volition?

Headshake.

"Alone or with somebody?"

Headshake.

"Or did something happen to her?"

Headshake.

"Why didn't you notify the police? Or did you?"

Headshake. This time the movement was violent enough to bring a pained sound out of his throat, to start blood trickling again from one nostril. His nose was swelling: burst-tomato blob, turning purple at the edges. He was still holding the stained towel; he lifted it up over the whole of his face, as if he were trying to hide behind it.

"Come on," I said, "we'll talk in the car."

I prodded him out onto the front deck, locked the door behind us. While I was doing that I removed the key from his case, slipped it into my pants pocket. Not for his sake, to keep him from refeeding his obsession; for mine, to allow me to get back in alone at some point. I was not done here, or with any of this business yet. There were too many questions that Victor Runyon probably couldn't or wouldn't answer. Too damned much confusion for me to walk away from it clean.

Chapter 7

WHEN WE WERE in the car and rolling, I said, "Talk to me, Mr. Runyon. What happened to Nedra?"

No response. I looked over at him as we passed under a streetlamp. He had his head tilted back against the seat, his eyes shut, the bloody towel cradled against his chest as if it were a security blanket. His breathing had a raspy regularity and I thought at first that he'd passed out. But as we neared Clarendon he stirred, groaned faintly, put the towel up to his leaking nose.

I said, "I'm going to keep asking you this until you give me an answer. What happened to Nedra Merchant?"

A few more seconds of silence. Then, "She went away."

"Went away where?"

"I don't know."

"You mean she disappeared?"

"Just . . . gone."

"Here one day, gone the next?"

"No, she . . . I don't know."

"Tell me about the last time you saw her."

"May ninth," Runyon said. "Saturday, May ninth."

"Where? Her house?"

"The house. Yes."

"She say anything then about going away?"

"No."

"How did she seem? Happy, sad, upset, afraid?"

"Angry," he said.

"Angry. Why was she angry?"

"We fought. A bad fight."

"Words, you mean? Or something physical?"

"Words. Just . . . ugly words."

"About what?"

"Us. She wanted to . . ."

"What, Mr. Runyon?"

"End it. End it once and for all."

"Your affair?"

"Our *love*," he said.

"Why did she want to end it?"

"Too possessive, she said. Smothering her."

Yeah, I thought.

"You asked her to marry you, is that it?"

"Yes. God, she knows how much I love her."

"But she didn't want to be tied down again."

"One bad marriage . . . it didn't have to be that way with us. I told her that. I love her too much; I worship her. But she wouldn't listen. She wouldn't listen."

"What happened then?"

No reply. I thought he'd gone away again, retreated behind the wall of his obsession—but he hadn't. When I asked him the question a second time his body jerked, as if with a sudden chill, and then he answered me in a thin, rusty voice, like hinges creaking in the dark.

"I left her alone. I went home."

"When did you try to talk to her again?"

"The next day."

"Called her? Went to see her?"

"Both. She . . . her machine was on. She wouldn't answer the door."

"But she was home that day, Sunday?"

"I don't know," Runyon said. "I'm not sure."

"Then what?"

"I kept trying . . . a few days, three or four."

"Calling her, trying to see her."

"Yes. Finally I went to her house, used my key. Then I knew she was gone."

"How did you know?"

"Felt it."

"Was anything disturbed?"

"I don't . . . disturbed?"

"Any signs of foul play?"

"No."

"Her car was missing but her clothes and other possessions were still there, everything exactly as it should be?"

"Yes."

"No message of any kind?"

"Message?"

"For you or someone else. Written or recorded."

"No."

"What did you think happened to her?"

"I thought she'd gone away for a while."

"Why did you think that?"

"Because of us, the fight we had. To think about us."

"Was she in the habit of doing that?"

"What?"

"Going away suddenly, unannounced," I said. "Disappearing for a few days, a week, longer."

"Once. She did that once, right after we met."

"How long was she gone that time?"

"A few days. She went to Tahoe."

"By herself?"

"Yes. She said she did that when she wanted to think."

"Always to Tahoe? Any special place up there?"

"No. I don't know."

"Okay. So at first you thought she went away to think things over—your proposal, your relationship."

"Yes," Runyon said. "Give it enough time, she'll change her mind. I know she will. She *has* to."

"You still believe that? That she's been holed up somewhere for nearly four months, trying to make up her mind?"

Silence. We were on Twin Peaks now, nearing upper Market; oncoming headlights sliced into the car, fragmented and threw splinters of light against his battered face. He had his head tilted back again but his eyes were open, blinking now and then against the glare.

"*Is* that what you believe now?"

"No," he said. "I don't believe that anymore."

"What do you believe?"

"I don't know what I believe. I do know she's alive, she's all right, she's not really hurt."

"Is it possible she went away with another man?"

"No," he said.

"Wasn't seeing anybody but you in May? Couldn't have broken off your affair because she'd met somebody new?"

"I told you why she wanted to leave me."

"Tell me about the man who attacked you tonight," I said.

Runyon coughed, spat thickly into the towel. His breathing had become more clogged from the swelling and the blood; it had a scratchy, wheezing cadence, like a man in the last stages of TB.

"Mr. Runyon? The man who attacked you—who is he?"

". . . I don't know his name."

"He knows yours."

"Don't know how he found out."

"Tonight isn't the first time you saw him face-to-face?"

"No. Twice before."

"Where? Nedra's house?"

"Both times. Just . . . showed up there."

"How long ago, the first time?"

"Three weeks."

Right, I thought. And after you left that night, he followed you home. Easy enough then for him to find out your name and telephone number.

"What did he say to you, that first time?"

"He wanted me to leave Nedra alone."

"Did he know she was missing?"

"No. He does now. He thinks I did something to her."

"You tell him she'd disappeared?"

"No. He found out."

"How?"

"I don't know."

"How long did it take him to find out?"

"Not long. A few days."

"Did he threaten you?"

"Veiled threats. Not like tonight."

"On the phone as well as in person?"

"Yes."

"Did he tell you his relationship with Nedra?"

"No. He . . . talks about her as if he owns her."

"A former lover?"

"Man like that? No. Nedra would never give herself to a man like that."

"Like what? A violent man?"

"Crude, uneducated. Ugly."

"She ever mention someone like him in her past?"

"No."

"Someone who'd bothered her, made trouble for her?"

"No."

"Would she have confided in you about that sort of thing?"

"Of course she would. We have no secrets."

Sixteenth Street coming up. That was the more direct route to S.F. General, over on Potrero, but I didn't take it; this time of night, it would be jammed around Mission Street with low-riders and the coffeehouse-and-disco crowds. I kept on going to Duboce and turned there.

I asked Runyon, "What have you done to try to find her?"

"Done?"

"You must have done something. Talked to friends, relatives—"

"She has no relatives. She's an orphan."

"Friends, then."

"No. Nedra is a private person."

"Everybody has at least one friend."

"Me," Runyon said. He was still wheezing, the words coming out with difficulty. "Lover and best friend. Now especially she needs no one but me."

Christ.

"People she works with, clients—you talk to any of them?"

"A few."

"None had any idea what happened to her?"

"Where she was, no. I didn't say she'd disappeared."

"Why the hell not?"

"I . . . couldn't. Too personal, too painful."

"What *did* you tell them?"

"I said she'd gone away for a while and I'd lost contact with her. I said she'd be back eventually. But they wouldn't listen, they were all so angry."

"Because of work she owed them?"

"Yes. No loyalty to her, no compassion."

"I don't suppose you contacted the police, the missing persons bureau?"

"No, I . . . I couldn't."

"Why couldn't you?"

"Have to be a relative to file a missing persons report. They couldn't find her anyway. If I couldn't reach her—the man who loves her, knows her best—how can strangers?"

Bullshit. You don't have to be a relative to file a missing persons report; all that's required is a personal or professional relationship with the individual and a willingness to detail it to the authorities. Maybe Runyon didn't know that, but he could have found out easily enough. He loved Nedra, he wanted to marry her, he was pathologically entangled with her . . . but still he hadn't quite been able to bring himself to uncover his ass and go public with his affair. And then he'd waffled too long and it was too late to do much of anything: he was hamstrung and any fresh leads to Nedra's whereabouts had gone stale, were probably lost for good by now. Weak and ineffectual personality, operating under a dangerous overload of indecision and worry and stress—that was Victor Runyon. Man caught and strangling slowly on the cord of his obsession.

"Just what exactly did you do, Mr. Runyon?"

"What?"

"To try to find Nedra."

"Everything I could think of. Went through her papers, her mail, her bills. Listened to her phone messages. Kept checking her favorite places . . . restaurants, shops, the aquarium, the De Young."

"That's all?"

"What else *could* I do?"

"You paid her past-due bills, didn't you?"

"Bills? Yes, I paid them."

"When they shut off the electricity at the house."

"Yes. I should have paid them sooner."

I didn't have to ask him why he'd done it. It was the same reason he'd built the shrine: an expression of sick, blind faith.

"She'll come back," he said thickly, "safe and sound. She has to, for both our sakes. You understand? She'll come back with me."

Like one of the disciples waiting for Christ to rise from the dead.

KAY RUNYON HAD ALREADY ARRIVED when I walked her husband into the emergency room at S.F. General. And she hadn't come alone; the other member of the family, Matt, was there too. When she saw Runyon's bruised and swollen face she bit her lip, hard; otherwise she showed no reaction. Neither did her son. Matt stood stone-faced, tense, his young-old eyes as bleak as the linoleum floor and the drab beige walls. Neither of them made a fuss or got in my way while I deposited Runyon on one of the benches.

I went to talk to an admissions nurse, tell her the nature of Runyon's injury. My footsteps echoed hollowly in the big room. Slack time, as early as it was and on a weeknight: only two other people in the waiting area, and both of those on silent vigils. No major-accident or gang-shooting victims so far tonight; no crack or heroin overdoses, no stabbings or bludgeonings or other serious trauma injuries. Even so, there was a charged atmosphere of expectancy among the staff: it was only a matter of time. I'd been here once on a particularly eventful Saturday night, and it had been like a combat-zone field hospital—the hurt and the dying lined out on benches and gurneys, hurrying paramedics and frazzled nurses and doctors in blood-spattered smocks. War is hell, and so is life in some parts of the city. In those parts, on certain nights, it amounts to the same thing.

When I got back to Runyon, his wife and son were sitting one on either side of him. Mrs. Runyon was saying something to him, but she might have been talking to herself for all the reaction she was getting. He didn't seem to know she was there. Kay Runyon, yesterday afternoon: *He just . . . retreated. Into himself, like a turtle pulling its head into its shell.* Yeah. He could bear his soul to me in all its raw, pathetic torment because I was a stranger and the contact was impersonal, without emotional baggage, like confiding to a priest in a confessional. Where his family was concerned it was just the opposite: too much emotional baggage, with the biggest chunk of it being guilt.

bare

I caught Kay Runyon's eye, gestured to her. She got up immediately and hurried over to me. The strain had hollowed out her cheeks even more, built little ridges of muscle around her mouth and along her jawline. But she was a strong woman, a hell of a lot stronger than her husband, and she had herself under rigid control. No tears tonight, not here and probably not in private.

I said, "Why did you bring the boy?"

"Matt knew something bad had happened," she said. "He could see it in my face. I couldn't lie to him. I told you yesterday, we don't have secrets."

Runyon in the car, talking about Nedra: *We have no secrets.* "Everybody has secrets," I said. "Besides, this isn't something a seventeen-year-old kid ought to know about his father."

". . . Is it that bad?"

"Pretty bad."

"Tell me."

"Not just yet. The nurse has insurance papers to be filled out. Can Matt do it?"

"Yes."

"Give him the job. Then we'll talk."

She moved away to talk to the admissions nurse. While she was doing that an intern came out with a wheelchair, and he and Matt helped Runyon into it. Runyon's face was a purple-and-red horror now, his nose swollen lopsidedly to three times its normal size. Whatever the boy felt looking at it, his own face betrayed nothing. He stood stoically as the intern wheeled his father out of sight.

I sat on a bench, away from everybody else, and watched Kay Runyon hold a low-voiced conversation with Matt. He argued with her but not for long; in less than a minute he took the insurance papers and sat down and began to scratch at them with a ballpoint pen.

She joined me again. Sat heavily, fumbled in her purse and came out with cigarettes and a lighter. I tapped her arm, pointed to a NO SMOKING sign on one wall. She said, "Shit," and put the cigarettes away. Then she said, "I hate hospitals. The smell . . . it's a death smell. Especially in a place like this. How can doctors and nurses work here?"

"Probably because to them it isn't a death smell," I said. "To them it's a life smell."

"I wish I cared about other people that much."

"You care, Mrs. Runyon."

"No, I'm selfish. I only care about my own." She drew a

thin, shuddery breath. "Who did that to Vic, hurt him like that? The man who's been calling?"

"Yes. I don't know his name yet, but I will tomorrow."

"Nedra? You found out who she is?"

I nodded and told her about Nedra Adams Merchant. All of it, full details and without trying to soften any of the facts. Bare knuckles don't hurt any more than blows encased in velvet. She had steeled herself for the worst, but there was no way she could have anticipated Nedra Merchant's disappearance or the scope of her husband's reaction to it. The news grayed her skin, added sickness to the pain in her eyes.

"I don't know him anymore," she said. "I don't know the Victor Runyon you're talking about."

"But he knows himself now, better than he ever did before. That's part of his problem. He knows and he can barely cope with the knowledge."

"He's still a stranger to me. I love the man I married, but I loathe and despise that stranger in there—I hate him as much as I've ever hated anyone. Does that make sense to you?"

"Some."

"Maybe I'm having a breakdown too," she said.

"I don't think so."

"Vic is. We both know that."

"Yes."

"What do I do about it? Talk to a psychiatrist?"

"I would. As soon as possible."

She nodded; it was a decision she'd already made and she'd wanted support for it. "But I can't force Vic to get help and I can't keep him chained at home. He'll go back to her house, you know he will. What if that man shows up and attacks him again?"

"There's something to be done about that. Once I know who he is I'll have a hard talk with him, threaten him with police action or a lawsuit. That might scare him off."

"What if it doesn't?"

"Then I'll talk to your husband, try to convince him to press assault charges."

"Suppose he won't? Then what?"

"Let's not get ahead of ourselves."

"What about Nedra? Do you have to report her disappearance to the police?"

"Reporting it isn't up to me, not unless I have evidence of foul play, kidnapping, some sort of crime."

"Is that what you think happened to her?"

"I don't have any opinions yet."

"Can you find out? Just you alone?"

"Three and a half months is a long time," I said.

"But it is possible."

"With some luck, yes."

"Will you try? If it turns out she's dead, if Vic is shown proof that she's gone for good, it might bring him to his senses. Don't you think so?"

"Maybe," I said.

"Will you do what you can? Please?"

"I'd already planned on it."

She started to thank me, but I didn't want to listen to that; she had nothing to thank me for. I cut her off by saying, "About your husband's car. Do you want me to drive you to Forest Hill so you can pick it up? Or drive your son?"

"No, not Matt. I don't want him to see where she lives. You can drive me. I'd just as soon leave the car where it is, but that won't keep Vic home. He'd only take a taxi."

"We can go now or in the morning."

"Now. I can't stand this place another minute. And I need a cigarette—God, I need a cigarette. Matt can drive his father home in my car."

KAY RUNYON DID NOT have much to say on the ride to Forest Hill. She sat stiffly, smoking one coffin nail after another in that quick, nervous way of hers. Even with my window down, enough of the smoke stayed in the car to irritate my lungs. But I endured it; I didn't have the heart to take away the one thing, even briefly, that gave her a measure of comfort.

When we rolled onto Crestmont she sat up straighter and peered intently through the windshield, like an animal entering hostile territory. And when I pulled over behind her husband's BMW she asked abruptly, "Which house is hers?"

I pointed it out.

"Very nice," she said. "I'm sure it's lovely inside. Does she have good taste in furnishings too?"

I didn't answer that. She didn't expect one anyway.

I kept the engine running, but Kay Runyon was not quite ready to get out of the car. She sat staring past me at the wood-shingled house across the street—and then she made a sound, low in her throat, a kind of rumbling. It took me a couple of seconds to identify it as bitter, humorless laughter.

"Vic found out some unpleasant things about himself," she said, "and now I'm finding out some unpleasant things about myself. I *don't* have much compassion. I'm as cruel and selfish as dear Nedra."

"Why do you say that?"

"I hope she's dead," Kay Runyon said. "I hope she died suffering; I hope she's been rotting in the ground somewhere for the past three and a half months."

Chapter **8**

THE FORD ECONOLINE VAN was registered to a Richard Rodriguez, with an address on Lowell Street in the city.

Harry Fletcher at the DMV had that information for me fifteen minutes after I opened the office on Friday morning. The balding guy hadn't struck me as a Latino, but appearances can be deceiving. So can the registered ownerships of vehicles; people who buy used cars don't always bother to reregister them, and people who drive a particular one aren't always their owners. Two other automobiles were registered in Rodriguez's name as well: a second, older Econoline van and a 1990 Olds Cutlass. Whoever Richard Rodriguez was, he believed in buying American. I asked Harry for the license numbers of the second van and the Olds, in case I needed them.

My next call was to TRW, to request a credit check on Rodriguez. Then I punched up the number of the AMA, to see if they'd come up with anything for me. They hadn't; no licensed psychiatrist named Duncan had practiced in San Francisco or anywhere in the Bay Area within the past ten years. The S.F. Bay Area Psychological Association had drawn the same blank where practicing psychologists and psychotherapists were concerned. Either the man Nedra Merchant had been seeing was unlicensed —some kind of head quack—or Lawrence April had in fact misremembered the name.

I put the Runyon-Merchant matter on temporary hold so that I could take care of the preliminaries on the department-store skip trace and then get some billing done. No bills sent, no checks received; and my cash flow was a little sluggish at the moment. I was working on the billing when the telephone went off.

Kay Runyon. Sounding tired and tense; she didn't have to tell me she'd had a sleepless night. She said, "He just called again."

"Who did?"

"The same man, the man who attacked Vic."

"You answered the phone?"

"Yes."

"He have anything to say to you this time?"

"God, I wish he hadn't. He asked for Vic and I recognized his voice and I—I lost it for a few seconds. I called him some names, I told him he wasn't going to get away with what he did last night. He just laughed."

"And said what?"

"He thinks Vic did something to Nedra . . . hurt her or drove her away, I don't know. I tried to tell him he was wrong. He kept saying somebody had better tell him where she was and she had better be all right. Or else. If I didn't know, then I'd better find out from Vic or have you find out for me."

"Me? He mentioned me?"

"Yes."

"By name or by profession?"

"Both. Didn't you tell him last night who you are?"

"No. Only that I was a friend of your husband's."

"But how . . . ?"

"I don't know. But I'll find out. Did he say anything else?"

"No. Then he hung up."

"How did he sound? His emotional state."

"Angry. Very angry."

"In control or not?"

"Yes, but . . . not underneath."

"Unstable?"

"Psychotic," she said.

Overreaction. Or was it? His frenzied assault on Runyon
. . . what was that kind of outpouring of rage if not a psychotic
episode? If I hadn't been there to pull him off, he might have
beaten Runyon to death.

But I was not about to admit that to her. I said, "Don't let
your imagination get the best of you. We'll have a better idea of
his mental state after I talk to him, do some checking into his
background."

"Do you know yet who he is?"

"I know who owns the car he was driving, yes. He may or
may not be the registered owner; I'll have that information pretty
soon."

"You'll call as soon as you know for sure?"

"As soon as I have anything definite," I said, and changed
the subject. "Your husband been up yet?"

"No. They gave him some pills at the hospital, for the pain
and to make him sleep. I made sure he took them when we got
home."

"You won't have to worry about him going out today. He'll
hurt too much when he wakes up to do anything but lie in bed. I
know; I've had my nose broken."

"He'll stay here," Kay Runyon said grimly, "if I have to
drug him and tie him to the bed."

"Have you contacted a psychiatrist yet?"

"I called six of them this morning. The earliest I could get
an appointment with anyone is next Tuesday. Tuesday, for God's
sake."

I didn't say anything.

"What does that tell you about the number of disturbed

people in this city?'' she said. ''About the society we live in? We're a nation of crazy people . . . we really are, you know.''

The conversation left me feeling bleak. And puzzled. It was possible that the balding guy had gotten my car license at the same time I'd gotten his last night. But how could he have known which car was mine? It was unlikely he'd noticed me drive up and stop; he had been too focused on Victor Runyon. And there'd been several other cars parked in the vicinity. And even if he had picked off my number, how could he have traced it so quickly? He wasn't a cop or another P.I., not the way he'd acted. I'd have sensed it right away if he were. You get so you can tell when you're dealing with one of your own kind.

The only other thing I could think of was that he'd recognized me, put the name to the face. My photograph has been in the newspapers and on TV, and not always for the right reasons. Not recently, though—and the photos available to the media hadn't been good likenesses.

So? How the hell *had* he found out who I was and what I did for a living?

THE OUTER MISSION is my old neighborhood. I was born and raised there, in a big rambling house just off Alemany Boulevard near the Daly City line. Lower middle-class, blue-collar neighborhood in those days, heavily ethnic European—Italians, Poles, Slavs, some Irish. Pretty good place to grow up in: the city was different back then, nurturing, the streets a far cry from the drug- and gang-riddled war zones they've evolved into today. Family and ethnic ties were rock-solid. We watched out for our own, policed our own—lived by codes and traditions that were centuries old—and kids like me, first-generation American-born, were better and stronger for it.

Not that my childhood was some kind of urban idyll. It wasn't. Loner then, loner now, shaped by circumstances as well as by genetic makeup. I played team sports, had a circle of casual friends; but I was close to only one, a tall gangly kid named Gino, and to none after he and his parents moved away when I was twelve. (Funny, I could no longer remember Gino's last name.) I was never a leader, never one of the popular ones; shy, clumsy, overweight kids seldom are. A tagalong, a fringer in every group and activity. So I preferred my own company, spending long afternoons in the walnut tree in the backyard, reading books and pulp magazines, living in a black-and-white fantasy world of heroes and villains, imagining myself as one of the good guys helping to right wrongs. More than anything else those childhood fantasy trips were why I went into police work, why I eventually turned to private investigation.

My home life hadn't been any bed of roses either. Nina, my sister and only sibling, died of rheumatic fever when she was five and I was eight. And my old man was a drunk, a verbal and sometimes physical abuser, a dockworker who couldn't hold a job and who got mixed up with a waterfront gang that was stealing goods out of the pier sheds and selling them on the black market. He drank himself to death at the age of fifty. I was seventeen then, six months shy of high school graduation. I didn't wait; I joined the army and went off to fight in the South Pacific, in another of humanity's mad wars. No one, not even Kerry, knows that I never finished high school; that I got into the MPs with the help of a friend in clerical who doctored my records, and into the police academy after I left the service on the strength of my MP training and record.

My old man's legacy might have left deeper, uglier scars if it hadn't been for Ma. She was a good woman, as good as anyone God ever made; a big, sad, loving woman from Genoa, who'd traded the old world for a new one she didn't like nearly as much, and who'd made the best of a life she didn't deserve. My old man killed her, too, with his drinking and his abuse, five years after he killed himself. She'd been a fine cook, like most Italian women of her generation, and the more he drank, the more she ate of her rich Genovese cooking for solace and escape. After he died she kept right on gorging herself for the same reasons, and because she was all alone in that rambling house. It was a heart attack that ended her life, induced by obesity and clogged arteries. She stood five-two and on the day she died she weighed two hundred and forty-seven pounds.

She taught me a lot of things, my ma. Love, empathy, patience, perseverance, self-sufficiency. Forgiveness, too, except where my old man was concerned. On her deathbed she'd begged me to forgive him his sins and excesses, and I'd said I would try; and I had tried, for her sake. But I couldn't do it. He'd lived and died a son of a bitch and he'd left me with nothing except contempt for his memory. I was Ma's son, not his—and thank Christ for that. I would not have been any good to anyone, least of all myself, if I'd grown into his kind of human being.

The house was gone now, long gone. I'd sold it after Ma died—too many mixed memories for me to want to live there— and the new owner had fallen asleep with a lighted cigarette one night in 1964 and burned himself and the house to cinders. What few homes of the same style and twenties vintage that still stood in the neighborhood today were tumbledown and graffiti-scarred, their porches enclosed by security gates, their windows barred, their once well-kept yards weed-choked or paved over with cracked concrete. The ethnic mix was much different too: Latinos, blacks, Asians. I barely recognized the neighborhood these days. Whenever business brought me out here I was a stranger in a strange land. Even so, the memories good and bad always seemed to come flooding back. . . .

Richard Rodriguez's address was a half block off Mission on Lowell. Two-story private house, newly painted and in better shape than its immediate neighbors, the lower floor converted into business premises. Over the business entrance was a sign that said RICHARD'S TV & APPLIANCE · SALES & SERVICE. Parked in the driveway was the older Ford van, this one painted midnight blue, with the same words on its sides that were on the sign. I didn't see the white van anywhere in the vicinity.

I parked and went inside under a jangling bell. One long, weakly lighted, low-ceilinged room, two thirds of which was packed with new and repaired television sets, VCRs, and the like; the other third, behind a short counter, was a work area. The man back there turned my way as I entered, letting me see a broad, dark face split by a cheerful smile. He wasn't the balding guy. He was in his mid-forties, Latino, with a full head of hair and a thick brush mustache.

"Morning," he said. He laid down the soldering gun he'd been using and came forward to the counter. "Nice day out there, huh?"

"Nice day," I agreed. "I'm looking for Richard Rodriguez."

"You found him. What can I do for you?"

"Do you own a white Ford Econoline van, Mr. Rodriguez?"

"That's right. Well, it's my wife's, but we put it in my name. Why?"

"Can you tell me who was driving it last night?"

"Why you asking?"

"Do you know a short, balding man with a reddish baby face?"

What was left of Rodriguez's smile upended itself into a disgusted scowl. "Ah, Christ," he said. "What's he done this time?"

"Who?"

"My wife's no-good brother. If he did something to the van, wrecked it or something—"

"What's your brother-in-law's name?"

"Cahill. Eddie Cahill. Listen, what's going on? Who are *you*?"

I showed him the Photostat of my license. His mouth worked itself into a sour-lemon pucker that conveyed even greater disgust. "I knew it," he said. "I knew he couldn't stay out of trouble."

"Cahill's been in trouble before?"

"Most of his miserable life. I told Marj; I said, you watch, inside of six months he'll be back in prison. He's got wires loose in his head, that *cholo*. But no, she don't want to believe it. Not about her baby brother."

"When was he in prison?"

"The last time? He got out about a month ago."

"Convicted of what?"

"Felony assault. He beat the hell out of some guy, damned near killed him. For no reason. Argument in a bar over baseball, can you believe it? *Baseball.*"

"When was that?"

"Couple of years ago. They gave him eighteen months."

"Which prison?"

"Lompoc."

"And you say he was in jail before that too?"

"Four years, in the early eighties."

"What was the rap that time?"

"Grand theft. He worked for a microelectronics outfit in San Jose. Him and another guy were stealing them blind."

"What's he been doing since he got out of Lompoc?"

"Doing?"

"Does he have a job?"

"Supposed to be working for me," Rodriguez said. "My wife talked me into it. Give him a chance to start over, she says. He knows electronics, doesn't he? she says. So he works two days and I haven't seen him since."

"He's had your wife's van since he got out?"

"Most of the time, yeah."

"Where's he living?"

"Daly City. Marj got him a cheap house rental."

"Mind giving me the address?"

"Castle Street, off Hillside. I don't know the number but it's in a bunch of row houses, they all look alike, take up half the block. Third one from the corner, across from an empty lot."

"Okay, thanks."

"What about the van?" he asked. "He didn't have an accident, did he? Or hit somebody with it? My insurance don't cover other drivers. . . ."

"No, no accident and no hit-and-run."

"What'd he do then? Why you looking for him?"

"He's been bothering some people I work for. Harassing them. First with telephone calls, then last night he attacked the man, broke his nose."

"Felony assault again," Rodriguez said. "Right back into prison, huh? I told Marj. I told her."

"Do you know a woman named Nedra Merchant? A graphics designer who lives in Forest Hill?"

"No. Why?"

"Your brother-in-law ever been in trouble over a woman?"

"Not that I know of. Is that why he broke some guy's nose? Over a woman?"

"Yes."

"I didn't think he cared about women that much," Rodriguez said. "I never saw him with one. Not him. Baseball, booze, electronics—that's all he ever talks about."

"He's never been married?"

"Never told Marj if he was. What're you gonna do when you find him? Arrest him?"

"I don't make arrests, Mr. Rodriguez."

"Have him arrested then? Send him back to prison?"

"That's not up to me."

"What's the guy with the busted nose gonna do? Isn't he gonna sign a complaint?"

"I don't know. Maybe not if your brother-in-law promises to leave him and his family alone from now on."

"I wouldn't bet on that. Eddie's got wires loose, like I said. And he's stupid-stubborn. He gets an idea in his head, you couldn't pull it out with a pair of pliers. You want my opinion?"

I shrugged. "Go ahead."

"Have his ass thrown back in prison," Rodriguez said, "any way you can manage it. That's where he belongs. That *cholo*'s no damn good. Just no damn good."

THE ROW HOUSE on Castle Street in Daly City was easy enough to locate. It was in a run-down, working-class neighborhood that seemed to be mostly the domain of Latin and other ethnic families.

But the trip out there was a waste of time. The white van wasn't there and neither was Eddie Cahill. And none of his neighbors knew where he was, when he'd be back, or anything about him.

Chapter 9

THE UNEASINESS STARTED as soon as I let myself into Nedra Merchant's house. Not because I expected any trouble; there was no sign of Cahill or the white van anywhere along Crestmont. And not because technically I was committing a felony trespass. The uneasy feeling was purely psychological.

I was an invader.

Entering a stranger's house without permission, no matter what the reason, always made me feel that way. Yes, it was the type of job I had; yes, I invaded the lives of strangers in some way nearly every day of my working life. But there is a difference between abstract intrusion and actual physical invasion, between telephonic and paper-trail snooping and laying hands like a burglar on personal and private belongings. In my mind there is, anyway. Even last night, with Victor Runyon on the premises, I hadn't felt right about prowling through the chambers of Nedra Merchant's home.

But you do what you have to do, like it or not. And if there were any cold-trail leads left to her whereabouts, this was the most likely place for them to be. The fact that Runyon had gone through her effects himself didn't mean much. He knew her, but he didn't know what to look for in a missing persons case. And his perception and judgment were clouded by his emotions.

I put the dead-bolt back on, pocketed Runyon's key. The family room drew me first. The sweet-decay scent of the flowers was stronger today; combined with the mustiness and the absence of light, it gave the room the dour aura of a mausoleum. I parted the drapes halfway, found sliding glass doors that gave access to the balcony outside, and opened one of those to let in some fresh air. Incoming sunlight slanted across Runyon's shrine, threw it into ugly and pathetic relief. It was the kind of creation that needed darkness and candle glow to give it symbolism and meaning. With the sun on it, there was no illusion: flowers wilted, candle wax pooled on the table like thick globs of dried black blood, even the silver frame exposed as tarnished goods. It was a dead thing, a dead monument to a dead love.

On impulse I gathered up all the flowers and what was left of the candles and took them out into the garage and dumped them into an empty garbage can. Then I went back into the room and carried Nedra Merchant's photograph to the window so that I could study it in the bright sunlight.

It was easy enough to see why men were attracted to her, why certain men could lose their heads over her. It wasn't that she was beautiful; her nose was too large, her mouth too wide, her chin a little too sharp for classic beauty. But there was a dark, sultry allure about her, enhanced by the long black hair and eyes that had an Oriental cast—one of the reasons she affected Asian dress and bedroom trappings, probably. The eyes seemed to radiate a smoky heat. Siren's eyes; witch's eyes. Not my type, Nedra Merchant, but I could feel the pull of those eyes even looking at them in a photograph. In person they would be magnetic.

I pried the cardboard backing off the frame, transferred the photo to my coat pocket. I might need it at some point; and if Victor Runyon did come back here soon, as it was probable he would—force his way in if he had to—he'd be better off if her likeness wasn't around to reinforce his mania. Then I prowled the room, opening drawers and cabinets, looking under sofa and chair cushions, flipping through magazines and books. None of that netted me anything. The kitchen, dining room, and formal living room held no clues either.

Downstairs to her office. On two walls were framed posters, one advertising a computer trade show, the other a local company that specialized in exotic varieties of coffee. Both were distinctive, striking, with accents on sharp angles, unusual typefaces, and splashes of primary color. Unsigned, but no doubt Nedra Merchant's work. The rest of the office was expensively but functionally furnished: desk in some kind of dark, burnished wood, leather armchair, computer terminal and printer, file cabinet and catchall table in the same dark wood as the desk.

Propped against the table was a drawing board, and on its top were some loose sketches, an artist's portfolio case, and two small cardboard boxes. I flipped through the sketches: more work in the same style as the wall posters. The contents of the case were samples of business brochures, company and trade magazines, posters of various sizes to be shown to prospective clients.

The cardboard boxes had been put there by Victor Runyon, evidently, because they contained her accumulated mail for the past three and a half months. One was filled with catalogs, flyers, and unopened letters; the other contained opened mail, a sheaf of papers clipped together, and two tiny cassette tapes.

I went through the larger box first. Junk mail, for the most part, plus several trade journals that she subscribed to or maybe had had a hand in designing, plus two packages from the Book-of-the-Month Club. Almost all of it had been addressed to a post office box downtown, near her office; she seemed to get little mail here at the house. There were no personal letters or postcards. No unpaid bills. The only items of interest were three Wells Fargo envelopes: her monthly checking account statements and cancelled checks. I slit each of those envelopes with my pocket knife. The oldest of the statements, dated the end of May, held some fifteen checks, most from late April and early May, none dated after May 7th. The statement for June contained a lone cancelled check, written on May 6th, to a wine shop in SoMa, and cashed too late to be included on the May statement. The statement for July had no cancelled checks. And none of the three showed any ATM cash withdrawals. Nedra Merchant's checking account balance had been $1,672.61 as of May 7th, factoring in the one late-cashed check, and it was still $1,672.61 three-plus months later.

All but one of the checks had been made out to banks, companies, stores. The exception was a check in the amount of $500 payable to Philip C. Muncon and endorsed on the back in a bold hand. Muncon, I thought. Muncon, Muncon . . . Duncan. Nedra's therapist? The names sounded alike; easy enough after five years for Lawrence April's memory to transform an uncommon name into a common one.

I moved over to the box of opened mail. No personal letters there either. And just one card, a birthday card signed "Aunt Louise." Plain card, without much sentiment. There was no return address on the envelope, but the postmark told me it had been mailed in Lubbock, Texas, on June 15. So Nedra Merchant's birthday was sometime around that date, and only one person in her life had cared enough to send her greetings.

The rest of the opened envelopes were Walter Merchant's three uncashed alimony checks; and bills, two and three each from utility companies, credit card firms, Saks Fifth Avenue and two expensive women's clothing shops. I checked the itemized charges on the credit card and store bills. None had been made after May 5th. The clipped-together papers were customer receipt portions of the most recent bills, with an inked notation on each of the date and amount paid by Victor Runyon. Careful records of his faith, to be presented to her like an offering on the day of her resurrection.

The cassette tapes would be for her telephone answering machine, I thought. All her messages preserved intact. I put those next to the machine for the time being and went to work on the desk.

Only one of the drawers, the largest on the bottom, had anything for me. Little hooks had been screwed into the wood along one side; keys hung from all but the last in line. Rectangles of adhesive tape, words written on each with a felt-tip pen, were affixed above each hook: *front door, side door, car, IID.* Spare keys for all the doors and locks in her life. The piece of tape above the empty hook said *Thorn.,* capital T and with a period after the last letter. Abbreviation of somebody's name—another lover, maybe? Or of a place?

I took the key off the hook marked *IID,* put it in my pocket, then went to the file cabinet. Personal records, exclusively: paid bills, receipts, cancelled checks and bank statements, income tax returns dating back several years. No business records; she probably kept those at Illustrative Image Designs. Not a single item of correspondence either. Apparently she wasn't a saver, even of what few cards and letters she did receive. If she wrote any letters, it was either by hand or on her computer; and if she'd saved any copies, they were on the discs stored in the bottom file drawer. If it turned out I needed to go through the PC files, I would have to bring in help. I don't know a damned thing about computers and I'm too old and too stubborn and too much of a technophobe to want to learn. My loss. Maybe.

One thing I did get out of the file cabinet: Philip C. Muncon was her therapist, all right. Had been for close to ten years. There was a thick file with his name on the tab—bills and cancelled checks dating back to the early eighties. That seemed a hell of a long time to be consulting one particular psychologist, but some people become dependent to the point of necessity—patients and doctors both. Muncon had been at the same address on Sacramento Street the entire ten years, which was a point in favor of his reputability. I copied the address and his phone number into my notebook.

Half-hidden by the answering machine was a Rolodex. I sat down in Nedra's leather chair and thumbed through it. Lots of names and addresses, but nearly all of them appeared to be business-related. There were no cards for Victor Runyon or Dean

Purchase or Lawrence April or Glen Grigsby or Walter Merchant; lovers past and present either weren't acknowledged this way or were erased completely from her life after they stopped being a part of it. Under *L* was one marked Aunt Louise, no last name, with an address in Lubbock, Texas, and a telephone number. Only one other card bore a female name: Annette Olroyd, with a local phone but no address. The information for both Aunt Louise and Annette Olroyd also went into my notebook.

Now the answering machine tapes. I rewound and played back the one that was already in the machine. Only two messages, both from prospective clients. Neither of the filled tapes was marked; I picked one and put it in to play. It was the older, dating back to early May. Clients who grew progressively angrier at not hearing from her; a charity solicitation; a soft and somewhat jittery female voice that identified itself as Annette; a husky male voice that said he was Philip Muncon and wanted to know if everything was all right, since she'd missed her appointment and it wasn't like her not to call. More business messages, the first dun call from a credit card company, another call from Annette—Annette Olroyd, I presumed—and a second from Dr. Muncon, both expressing concern because Nedra hadn't gotten in touch with them. End of tape.

I switched it for the second full one. Philip Muncon had telephoned a third time, urging Nedra to call or visit him as soon as possible because he was "quite worried" about her. But that was the last message from him, left in early June; I knew the approximate date because a client who rang up afterward gave the date of his call as June 13th. Why nothing more from Muncon? And why no further messages from Annette Olroyd? Had Nedra contacted one or both of them, offered an explanation that put their minds at ease?

The last half of the tape had some interesting messages. Two were from Walter Merchant, who had told me about calling his ex-wife. Both were straightforward, businesslike, and didn't say much other than that he'd appreciate hearing from her. Then—

"Hello, Nedra. You know who this is, baby?" The man must have assumed she did know, because he didn't identify himself. He didn't have to as far as I was concerned; Eddie Cahill's voice was reasonably distinctive. "I'm back and I'm gonna be around for a long time now. I just wanted you to know I'll be seeing you. Soon. Real soon. Bye for now."

Cahill had called again, just how soon afterward I couldn't tell; but it was the last message on the tape. His tone in the first had been smarmy; his tone in the second had an edge of anger. "I know all about you and Vic the architect. You better get rid of him, sweetheart. And you better not sic that lawyer on me again. I'm warning you on both counts."

I rewound the tape, replaced it with the mostly blank one, and then got up for another look in the file cabinet. Her attorney's name was James Keverne; I'd glanced through his file earlier. All the papers had seemed to pertain to her divorce, but I should have paid closer attention: At the rear was a handful of documents that dealt with Edward R. Cahill, including a copy of a restraining order issued by a San Francisco judge two years ago. Evidently Cahill had spent six weeks harassing Nedra Merchant with telephone calls, several of which she'd taped, in which he'd made "overt sexual advances and veiled threats"; and on two occasions he'd accosted her in public before witnesses, the second time "causing her to fall while attempting to flee, the result of this fall being minor injuries requiring medical attention." Going by what Richard Rodriguez had told me, the restraining order had been issued around the time Cahill was arrested on the unrelated charge of felony assault that sent him to Lompoc.

James Keverne's name, phone number, and Fremont Street address made a fourth notebook entry. After which I put everything back the way I'd found it and went to sift through the rest of the downstairs rooms.

I came up empty-handed there. But there was no disappointment in that. The leads I'd turned up in Nedra's office had already exceeded my expectations.

* * *

ILLUSTRATIVE IMAGE DESIGNS, INC. was housed in a two-story brick building above a printing company on Third and Harrison. You went up two flights of stairs from the street and down a short hallway, to where two doors faced each other like a couple of old adversaries. A pair of converted lofts, I thought. The front one, facing Third, belonged to a combination art school and gallery that specialized in something called post-1900 Russian constructivism. The door to the back loft bore the name of Nedra Merchant's company and yielded to the key I'd taken from her desk.

Nobody had been here in a long time. It smelled of dust and disuse, like a closed-up attic room; dust coated the furnishings, swam in wedges of sunlight that penetrated through a pair of mesh-screened skylights. She'd set the loft up to serve as a showplace as well as an office and workroom. Posters, two- and four-page brochures, magazine covers, and design layouts papered the walls, and there was a big artist's file with long, flat drawers that contained a great many more samples of her handiwork. Also present were a computer, several drawing boards, a table loaded down with pens and brushes and paints and other tools of her trade. A cabinet held all of her business records: invoices, correspondence, preliminary plans and sketches for various projects. There wasn't a whisper of her personal life in any of it. Nor in any other part of the loft. This place was strictly for business. And if there was any connection between Illustrative Image Designs and her disappearance, I couldn't find it.

I locked up again and went over to the art school and gallery, where a young guy wearing a bushy beard and a ponytail gave me a big rush until he found out I wasn't interested in buying post-1900 Russian constructivism or in taking lessons in how to create it. Then he lost interest. My questions about Nedra Merchant—I used the insurance background check dodge to explain myself—didn't revive it much.

"I hardly know the woman," he said with a faint, arrogant sneer. "We say hello when we run into each other, that's all. We have little in common. I'm an artist and she . . . well, she's

very successful, I'm sure, with her commercial pap for the indis-
criminate eye.''

Whereas his discriminate eye had not even noticed that
she'd been absent and her office closed up tight for nearly four
months. Real artists are *so* sensitive, *so* in touch with the world
around them. Yes they are.

JAMES KEVERNE WAS STILL out to lunch, even though it was
after two o'clock. Feasting with his secretary, maybe; the only
person in his office was a harried-looking paralegal. Yes, he was
due back at some point, but she wasn't sure just when. Yes, she
would give him my card and ask him to call me as soon as it was
convenient. Yes, she would tell him it concerned a client of his
and a two-year-old restraining order.

I drove from his office to mine. Three messages: Joe
DeFalco, one of Dean Purchase's secretaries, Barney Rivera.
DeFalco wanted to know how things were going with Kay Runyon; and why didn't we get together for a drink tonight, he had a
funny story to tell me about Eberhardt. To hell with him and to
hell with his funny story. Purchase's secretary said Mr. Purchase
would be free from 3:45 to 4:00 this afternoon and would see me
then in his office; if that was convenient, would I please call back
to confirm? I thought about it, asking myself again if I really
needed to talk to Dean Purchase. The answer was the same as
before. After all, he was willing to give me fifteen minutes of his
valuable time, wasn't he? I called his secretary back and confirmed.

Barney Rivera is Great Western Insurance's chief claims
adjustor and, like DeFalco, an old poker buddy. When a job
comes up that requires investigative work, Barney as often as not
calls me first—Great Western, as is the case with most small
insurance companies, doesn't have enough need or funds to em-
ploy a staff investigator. I called him as soon as I was done with
Purchase's secretary. When Barney dangles a bone you take it
quick; his bosses demand fast service and there were any number

of other free-lance detectives waiting in line to give it to them. Eberhardt, for one.

The job he had to offer was routine: A married couple wanted to insure each other's life for $250,000, with a double-indemnity clause for accidental death, and Great Western wanted to make sure there were no ulterior motives involved before they sold the policy. I said I'd handle it and Barney gave me the particulars. Then he said, "You been burning the midnight oil lately, huh? Lot of night work?"

"Not really. Why?"

"Neglecting Kerry, though, right?"

"She's the one neglecting me," I said.

"Yeah? Been doing a lot of night work herself, has she?"

"Now that she's creative director at Bates and Carpenter."

"Some night work's more creative than other kinds."

"What's that supposed to mean?"

"I ought to know," he said slyly. "Night work's my specialty."

"You going to start bragging again?" Rivera is a roly-poly little bugger with a passion for peppermints and an inexplicable attraction for the maternal type of woman. He seldom lacks for female companionship; to hear him tell it he's the Warren Beatty of the insurance racket. "It's too early in the day for tales of lust and perversion."

"You think so? Well, I happened to be squiring a sweet young thing last night and she's the kind that likes to be plied with dinner, drinks, and a little nightlife before she's ready to do the nasty. One of the places we stopped in was Henry the Eighth's, over on Clay, about ten o'clock."

"So?"

"Who did I see there but your lady love."

"So?"

"She wasn't alone. She was with a gentleman."

Barney has his share of faults and one of them is a mildly sadistic sense of humor. One of the other regulars at our monthly poker game had dubbed him Barney the Needle. "I repeat—so?"

"Doesn't bother you, huh?"

"Why should it? She was with one of her clients."

"Didn't look like a business meeting to me. Looked like hanky-panky. They were snuggled up in a booth, drinking wine and gazing soulfully into each other's eyes."

"Oh Christ, Barney, cut it out, will you?"

"Saw her kiss him once, right on the mouth," he said. "Now that's what I call creative directing."

He'd succeeded in rankling me. "All right, that's enough."

"You think I'm kidding?"

"I think you're full of crap, that's what I think."

"Could be, but I saw what I saw. And she didn't see me. Too busy with the, ah, client."

"Shut up, Barney."

"You want to know what he looked like?"

"No. I told you—"

"About her age, handsome, little silver at the temples. Complete opposite of you. Slender, for one thing. Well dressed, for another—the *GQ* type."

"You son of a bitch!"

"Trouble in paradise, paisan'?"

I hung up on him. Sat there for about ten seconds, not thinking anything, not feeling anything. Then I said, "Bullshit," aloud. And picked up the receiver again and called Bates and Carpenter. Usually I put my calls there through the switchboard and Kerry's secretary, so as not to disturb her if she's busy; this time I rang her private number.

She was in and she was busy; she sounded as frazzled and preoccupied as she had yesterday. "You caught me at a bad time," she said. "I'll call you back a little later—"

"I won't keep you long, babe," I said. "I just wanted to know if we can get together tonight. I really need to see you."

"Oh . . ." And a little silence. And: "Not tonight. I just can't. I've *got* to do some more work on the Blessing account."

"That the account you were working on last night?"

"Yes."

"What happened to Granny's Bakeries?"

"I passed the buck. It was either that or shove Granny Bridger out a window."

"How late did you work?"

"Until about ten."

"Missed your pro-choice meeting, then."

"Yes."

"What did you do after you left the office?"

"What do you think? I went straight home to bed."

"Kerry, listen—"

"I really do have to go," she said. "Talk to you later, okay?"

And she was gone and I sat there, holding the dead phone, listening to the after-echoes of her voice and to the dull, heavy beat of my heart.

Chapter 10

NOT KERRY, DAMN IT. Not Kerry!

I didn't want to believe it . . . and yet she'd lied to me. She wasn't a liar, hadn't once told me an untruth in all the years we'd been together; I was sure of that. Our relationship was built on trust as well as love. So why should she lie to me now unless she had something to hide, something like an affair with another man?

Barney Rivera wasn't a liar either. A bastard with a malicious streak, but not a liar. If he said he'd seen her with a man at Henry the Eighth's at ten o'clock last night, then he'd seen her. If he said they'd been snuggling in a booth, drinking wine and gazing into each other's eyes, then they had been. If he said Kerry had kissed the man on the mouth, then she had.

Trouble in paradise, paisan'?

I slammed my fist down on the desk, did it again—hard blows that made things jump and run and tumble to the floor. The ceramic mug of Jimmy Carter that I kept my pens and pencils in shattered. My hand began to sting, to hurt all the way up to the elbow; I stared at the red mark along the edge of my palm.

And the anger went out of me as suddenly as it had come, was replaced by a dull anxiety.

Stupid, hitting the desk that way. What if I'd broken my damn hand along with Jimmy Carter? I got down on my knees and picked up the shards and the pens and pencils and other items I'd dislodged. Shards into the wastebasket, other stuff back on the desktop.

I was sweating.

I went down the hall to the bathroom cubicle and splashed cold water on my face. It made me feel better, helped to reshape my thinking. Jumping to conclusions . . . you ought to know better than that. Benefit of the doubt, innocent until proven guilty. Remember when you thought she was having an affair with one of her bosses? Nothing to the Jim Carpenter thing, was there? Big false alarm, right? Same thing here.

She didn't lie and Barney didn't lie: half-truths, exaggerations, misconceptions. She'd been at Henry the Eighth's with a client, she'd kissed him on some impulse or other—that was all there was to it. Worked late, stopped for a drink, nothing wrong in that, but she hadn't wanted to admit it because she felt guilty about neglecting me or didn't want me to get the wrong idea. What was the sense in making myself crazy over a minor incident, an innocent misunderstanding?

Goddamn Barney and his frigging needle . . .

The telephone was ringing when I walked back into the office. Good—get my head back into business. James Keverne? No, a small surprise: Walter Merchant.

"I've been wondering," he said, "how you're making out with your investigation."

"Yes? Why is that, Mr. Merchant?"

"Curiosity."

"You told me yesterday that you're over your ex-wife."

"I am. But I do have a certain vested interest—those uncashed alimony checks of mine. Have you found out yet why Nedra didn't cash them?"

"She hasn't been around to cash them," I said. "She vanished three and a half months ago. Suddenly and without a trace.''

Silence.

"Early May," I said. "Sometime around the ninth."

"Jesus," he said in a hushed voice.

"You have any idea what happened to her?"

"Me? Good God, how would I know? I told you, I haven't seen Nedra in nearly a year."

"You also told me you hadn't been in touch with her in six months. But you called her house at least twice recently and left messages on her answering machine."

"How did you—" He cut that off and I could hear him suck in a heavy breath. "Never mind that. All right, I called her. I wanted to find out why she hadn't cashed those checks. Now I know the answer."

"Why did you lie to me?"

"It didn't seem like much of a lie. I suppose . . . well, I didn't want to get involved in whatever mess she was in. Mess I thought she was in at the time—some kind of triangle situation. This . . . her disappearing . . . that's a whole different can of worms."

"Yes, it is. Any theories?"

"No. I wouldn't want to speculate. I just hope—" Another heavy breath. "Three and a half months is a long time to be missing without a trace."

"You probably know her better than anybody. Is she the type to go off by herself, hole up somewhere for that length of time? For any reason?"

"No," Merchant said. "Not Nedra. The only two things she cares about in this world are men and her work. She wouldn't quit either one for four days, let alone nearly four months."

"Would she give up her work here for a man? Go off with him, start fresh in another location?"

"No."

"You're positive? People change in five years."

"Not Nedra."

"Do you know a man named Eddie Cahill?"

"Cahill . . . no. Who's he?"

"An ex-con who harassed her so badly two years ago she got a restraining order against him."

"Not one of her lovers? I can't imagine Nedra taking up with an ex-convict. . . ."

"Probably not." I described Cahill. "Familiar?"

"No. I don't know him."

"Nedra never told you about the harassment?"

"I wish she had."

"Annette Olroyd. You know her?"

"Who?"

"Olroyd. Annette Olroyd."

"The name's not familiar."

"How about Aunt Louise in Lubbock, Texas?"

"Nedra's aunt, yes. But if you think Nedra went to see her, or she knows what happened to her, you're wrong."

"Why is that?"

"They aren't close; they hadn't seen each other in fifteen years when Nedra and I were married. They never even talked on the phone. Cards on birthdays and Christmas, that was all. The woman must be in her eighties now. Besides, Nedra hates Texas." Sardonic little chuckle. "I think one of her less success-ful conquests was a Texan."

"The abbreviation 'Thorn.'—does that mean anything to you? First part of a word or name like Thornhill or Thornbridge, possibly."

"I don't think so. Why?"

"She had a spare key hook in her desk marked T-h-o-r-n period. The key is missing too."

"A man's name?"

"That's what I'm trying to find out."

"I can't help you. It's meaningless to me."

"If anything occurs to you," I said, "anything at all that might help me locate her, will you let me know?"

"Yes, of course. You *are* looking for Nedra, then? I mean, that's why you were hired?"

"Not initially. Now . . . yes, I'm looking for her."

"The police—have they been notified?"

"No. No one's filed a missing persons report yet."

"Good God, why not?"

"Only one person had any real knowledge that she'd disappeared until I found out last night, and he wasn't in a position to report it. That's all I can tell you."

"Then I'll do it," he said grimly.

"You can if you like, Mr. Merchant. But you said yourself, three and a half months is a long time. The police aren't going to be able to follow a cold trail any better than I can—and I've already got a running start."

"If you find out anything definite, then what?"

"That depends on what I find out. If I think the police need to be brought in for any reason, I'll notify them myself. Immediately."

"And me? Will you notify me, too, as a favor?"

"I don't see why not."

"*Anything* definite."

"Yes."

"All right. We'll leave it that way for now."

I held the disconnect bar down, the receiver tucked into the hollow between my neck and shoulder, and fished out my notebook and then tapped out Annette Olroyd's number. A dozen rings, no answer. Aunt Louise in Texas? There didn't seem to be much point in contacting her, after what Merchant had told me. Let it go for now.

I cradled the receiver and sat listening to the sounds of silence.

Kerry, I thought.

No, I thought—and got up and got moving.

DR. PHILIP MUNCON'S OFFICES were on the corner of Sacramento and Spruce streets in the Laurel Heights district. Upscale neighborhood, this, a mix of residences, small businesses—antiques shops, boutiques, trendy restaurants—and medical and professional services. Some of the various doctors were housed in the California Pacific Medical Center, others in converted Edwardians and Queen Anne row houses.

Muncon had the entire upper floor of his narrow Queen Anne. It was not exactly a posh layout, but you knew as soon as you walked in that his services would not come cheap. Wall-to-wall carpeting, comfortable furniture with an abundance of pillows, muted color scheme; at least a pair of consultation rooms and a private office, in addition to the reception area; and a smiley male receptionist with the most perfectly styled hair I'd seen on a person of either sex.

The doctor was with someone—the receptionist used the word "client"—but the session would be finished in another fifteen minutes. I sat and waited and wondered what it would be like, coming here one or more times a week for ten years to air your troubles and have them analyzed down to the minutest detail. I couldn't imagine it. The whole concept of therapy was foreign to me. I could understand why some people might need short-term counseling, somebody to help them get at the root of a particular problem—but I was not one of them. Too self-aware, too in touch with my weaknesses and shortcomings. I either solved my problems on my own or devised compromises so I could live with them. A shrink might have said that that was a self-delusional attitude, but I was not about to pay one hundred dollars-plus an hour to hear him say it, so it was a moot point. Call me a benign agnostic where therapy was concerned. I might not believe in it for myself, but I respected the ones who sought help when they needed it. Too many of society's ills could be laid at the feet of those who didn't.

At the end of fifteen minutes a middle-aged woman in a chartreuse pants suit came out of one of the consultation rooms. She didn't look happy; maybe Muncon had told her—rightly, if so—that chartreuse not only wasn't her color, it made her look like one of the victims in a green-slime horror flick. The receptionist took my card and the reason for my visit in to the doctor. He was gone a long time; evidently Muncon was trying to decide whether or not to grant me an audience. The decision, when it finally came, was in my favor, though probably not by much.

Muncon's private office was small, cluttered, and ripe with the scent of the tweedy cologne he used. Muncon himself was about fifty, distinguished-looking, with a heavy blue-black beard shadow and penetrating hazel eyes. The eyes didn't blink while he was talking to you. The entire upper two thirds of his face remained motionless, in fact; only his mouth moved—wide and thin-lipped, so that it made me think of a clam opening and closing.

He was a clam in the informational department as well. The first thing he said to me was "You understand that client-doctor confidentiality forbids me to discuss my professional relationship with Ms. Merchant."

"Yes, I do. I'm not going to ask you to reveal anything of a confidential nature."

"Just what are you going to ask me?"

"To begin with, if you're aware that Nedra Merchant is missing."

"Missing?"

"For the past three and a half months. Since sometime around May ninth."

The penetrating eyes were like surgical lasers. I looked away, looked back quickly to see if I could catch him blinking. No. Maybe he never blinked; maybe, like a bird, he had some physiological quirk that kept his eyeballs perpetually moist.

At length he said, "You're mistaken."

That made *me* blink. "I am? You mean she's not missing?"

"Away from the city, yes. Missing, no."

"You've seen her recently?"

"Not recently."

"Since May ninth?"

"No, not since early April."

"You've talked with her, then?"

"She has communicated with me," Muncon said.

"By telephone? By letter?"

"By card."

"What kind of card?"

"Postcard."

"Just one, or more?"

"Two, as a matter of fact."

"In her handwriting?"

"Certainly."

"When did you receive the most recent one?"

"Late last month."

"I don't suppose you'll tell me what they said."

"No. But I will tell you that Ms. Merchant is healthy, in good spirits, and plans to return to San Francisco shortly."

"How short is shortly?"

A faint, noncommittal smile.

"Why did she go away without telling anyone? Why hasn't she communicated with her clients or the man she'd been having a relationship with?"

"She has her reasons," Muncon said.

"Reasons that satisfy you?"

"Yes."

"You weren't satisfied when you called her home in May and June and left messages on her answering machine."

"I hadn't heard from her. I didn't know the reasons."

"Where were the postcards mailed?"

The faint smile again. "I'm sorry," he said.

"At least give me a general geographical location."

"I'm afraid not. Ms. Merchant specifically asked me not to reveal her whereabouts."

"Uh-huh," I said. He was starting to irritate me. Irrationally, maybe, but I have never reacted well to people with supercilious attitudes. And why the hell didn't he blink? "Tell me this: Does the abbreviation 'Thorn.' mean anything to you? Short for Thornhill, Thornwood, Thornbridge—something like that."

"No. Should it?"

"Whatever or whoever 'Thorn.' is, she had a key with that name attached to it. The key is also gone."

This time he shrugged and said nothing.

"Eddie Cahill," I said.

"Yes?"

"Does that name ring any bells?"

The smile, the penetrating stare. Then, meaningfully, he looked at a thin gold watch on his left wrist. "I have a client coming at four," he said. "It's a quarter of now. I'm afraid I'll have to terminate our conversation."

"Sure thing," I said. I got to my feet. "Just one more question. You wouldn't happen to be one of Nedra's lovers yourself, would you?"

It didn't faze him. "In addition to my work here," he said evenly, "I am involved in several programs to promote AIDS research. I live in the Castro and worked as a fund-raiser on Harry Britt's last campaign for supervisor. My housemate's name is Charles. Do I make myself clear?"

"Perfectly clear."

I went out feeling frustrated. And still irritated; the fact that Dr. Philip Muncon was gay didn't make him any less supercilious and uncooperative. Or excuse the fact that he didn't blink.

As of late last month, Nedra Merchant was healthy, in good spirits, and planning an imminent return to San Francisco? She had reasons for suddenly disappearing, for abandoning her work and her life-style for almost four months, that satisfied her shrink? Yes, it was possible. No, I didn't doubt that Muncon had told me the truth as far as he knew it. Yes, Nedra Adams Merchant was a stranger to me—I had no idea of what motivated her or what might have driven her away from the city in early May.

But *I* wasn't satisfied. Not at all.

Gut feeling: Something bad, very bad, had gone and maybe was still going down.

Chapter  **11**

DEAN PURCHASE WAS A BIG MAN physically as well as politically: a wide-body with beefy shoulders, thick waist, powerful legs and thighs, and not too much overlay of fat for a man of fifty-odd. Mane of silver-black hair that was more judicial than senatorial. He dressed conservatively except for his ties. Outlandish ties were his trademark; he'd been cultivating them so long that a local TV station had once done a feature on his collection and private citizens sent him the ugliest and most tasteless ones they could find. The one he had on today was a sort of robin's-egg blue with bright red and yellow whorls and bright orange interlocking circles. Stare at it long enough and it might put you into a hypnotic trance. If it didn't make you sick to your stomach first.

I walked into his offices at city hall at 3:40, and at exactly 3:45 he came out of his private sanctum, looked me over, smiled at me as if I were a campaign contributor, pumped my hand, and ushered me inside. I'd been wondering which of his public personas I'd get. He had several: Tammany Hall Jovial, Mr. Hard-Ass, Mr. Sincerity, Man-of-the-People, Hardline Liberal, It's-a-

Tough-Job-but-Somebody's-Got-to-Do-It, The Humanitarian, The Fund-Raiser, The Comedian, The Confidant, The Bargainer. He could switch from one to another with the deceptive speed of a quick-change artist, as the situation called for; and watching him do it, you wondered if he had a real self left under all those public faces. Or if he—hell, most politicians these days—existed only as a public figure, in the eyes of his beholders. Was in effect just an animated hunk of clay in private, like a New Age state-of-the-art ventriloquist's dummy waiting to be activated by the presence of an audience.

Purchase's inner sanctum was big enough to have a cozy little sitting area at one end, complete with a couch and some leather chairs. He invited me to sit, offered me coffee "or something stronger," and when I declined on both counts, poured himself a cup of coffee so dark it had the color of india ink. Then he plunked himself down companionably in the chair next to mine.

"New Orleans blend," he said, indicating the cup. "Not too heavy on the chickory. Sure you won't try it?"

"No, thanks."

"Well," he said, and sipped, and said, "Ah," and smiled again. He did Tammany Hall Jovial well, but it was wearing thin on me; I hoped he would segue into one of the others pretty soon. Even Mr. Hard-Ass would be preferable.

I said, "You're a busy man, Mr. Purchase, and so am I, so let's get right to the point. I'm not here to do you any harm. If you've checked me out—and I'm sure you have—you know I have a long-standing reputation for discretion, honesty, and straightforward business practices. Your name came up in a case I'm working on. As far as I know, the case has nothing to do with you; but there's a chance you may know something that will help me get to the bottom of it, so I'd like to ask you some questions. Whatever you say to me is strictly between us—it goes no farther than this office."

"Well stated." Purchase's smile was gone now; he'd adopted a serious, attentive mien. The Confidant. He set his mug down, leaned closer. "You wrote Nedra Merchant's name on your card. Is she your client?"

"No. She's involved with a party connected with my client."

"I see. Are you investigating her, then? Gathering evidence against her for some reason?"

"Not at all. I don't intend her harm in any way. Nor does my client."

"Then why are you interested in my relationship with her, such as it is?"

"I'm not. But I have reason to believe you know her fairly well, and I—"

"Who led you to believe that, may I ask?"

"Confidentiality, Mr. Purchase."

"Yes, of course. But I'd like to know what your confidential source alleged was the nature of my relationship with Ms. Merchant."

"That it was personal."

"Sexual?"

"Personal. *Was* it sexual?"

"It was not. Nedra and I were friends, nothing more."

"Were? You're not any longer?"

"I haven't seen her in quite some time," Purchase said. "We no longer move in the same circles."

"How long a time?"

"Nearly two years."

"And how long did you know her before that?"

"A few months. We met at a political fund-raiser."

"Did you spend much time together?"

"Not much, no. I took her to dinner twice, as I recall. And with my wife's knowledge and consent, I might add."

"Did you and Nedra discuss personal matters?"

"What sort of personal matters are you referring to?"

"Her private life. Did she confide in you?"

"You'll have to be more specific than that."

"For instance, the names of men she was intimate with—"

"No. That topic never came up."

"Her plans for the future? Places she liked to visit, where she went when she wanted to get away for a while?"

"I don't recall discussing those topics."

"Has she ever sent you postcards?" I asked.

The question caught him off guard. "Postcards?"

"Picture postcards. When she was away on a trip."

"Hardly. Nedra?" He frowned. "Why do you ask that?"

"I thought you might have heard from her recently."

"Well, I haven't. I told you, I've had no contact with the woman in nearly two years."

"Does the abbreviation 'Thorn.' mean anything to you?"

"Thorn?"

"The first part of a word like 'Thornbridge.' "

"No," Purchase said. He tugged at his lower lip. "What does that have to do with Nedra?"

"It might help me find her."

"Find her?"

"She's been missing since early May."

"I don't . . . missing? My God, you mean something's happened to her?"

"It's a strong possibility."

"She simply . . . vanished? Without a trace?"

"Minute traces, that's all."

"And you're trying to find her after all this time?"

"Among other things, yes," I said. "I'm not at liberty to discuss the circumstances of my investigation. Confidentiality, as I said before. But I am interested in knowing why she left the city so suddenly and where she is now."

"The police? Have they been told?"

"Not yet."

"But they will be?"

"Unless I can track her down myself, within a reasonably short period of time."

He tugged at his lower lip again; I could almost hear his thoughts grinding together. "If they are called in," he said at length, "I would be in your debt if you didn't give them my name. If I could help in any way, of course I would; but I can't. And you know how the media can distort the most innocent situation, make it into something sordid."

"Uh-huh."

"I'd be very grateful. I mean that."

Now he was Mr. Sincerity. And The Bargainer, covering his tail. If I balked even a little, and he perceived me as a threat, he'd become Mr. Hard-Ass in a twinkling.

I said, "If it's not necessary to give the authorities your name, Mr. Purchase, then I won't do it. Fair enough?"

I thought he might argue the point; he wanted a firm commitment. But he didn't argue. Maybe his intelligence reports had stressed the fact that I wasn't somebody who could be intimidated or bought off. Or maybe he was just being circumspect.

"Fair enough," he said, and put an end to our little interview by getting to his feet and holding out his hand. I stood, too, shook the hand even though I didn't much feel like touching him again. "I hope you find Nedra safe and sound. She's a fine person; I was proud to have her as a friend."

I nodded without speaking.

"If there's anything I can do—privately, just between you and me—don't hesitate to call on me. Will you do that?"

"Count on it, Mr. Purchase."

I went out of there thinking that he was a slimy son of a bitch. And that he had yet another persona among his repertoire, one that he'd slipped in and out of the whole time we were talking—particularly where his relationship with Nedra Adams Merchant was concerned.

The Liar.

THIS TIME, when I took myself out to Castle Street in Daly City, Eddie Cahill was home. Or at least the white Ford van was there, parked in front of the third row house from the corner.

I pulled up across the way, next to the weed-clogged vacant lot. It was colder out here, windier, with low-riding clouds that worked with the sun to create a light-and-shadow show. I sat for a few seconds, watching the run-down neighborhood alternately turn from pale gold to dull gray, getting my mind clear on what I wanted to say to Cahill. Then I crossed the street and went along a cracked walk and banged on the door of his rented row house, the way authority knocks.

He opened up pretty quick. Not much reaction when he saw me; just a facial tightening along the jaw and under the cheekbones, until the skin in those places was tight as a drumhead. The blue eyes had malice in them. He was wearing Levi's jeans and a white knit pullover that showed off muscle-knotted arms and well-developed pecs. Lifted weights in prison, I thought. The knuckles on his right hand were wrapped in a thin, crude bandage: badge of dishonor from last night's attack on Victor Runyon.

"Well," he said, "the private cop," and came out to stand at a little distance from me on the walk, leaving the door open. I could read his mind plainly enough. If there was going to be trouble, he wanted room to maneuver.

"How'd you know I was a private investigator?"

Crooked yellow grin. "What do you want, slick?"

"It's not what I want, Cahill, it's what you want."

"Yeah? What's that?"

"Not to go back to prison."

No response. But the grin died fast.

"You've been in twice," I said. "You go back again and it'll be hard time—Quentin or Soledad instead of Lompoc. A second fall for felony assault and a third felony conviction ought to net you a minimum of five years, even with plea bargaining. You don't want to do another nickel behind bars."

"Bullshit," Cahill said.

"I saw you bust up Victor Runyon, remember? I'll testify that it was an unprovoked attack, if it comes to that. So will Runyon," I lied. "He's already agreed to press charges if you don't leave him and his family alone."

"He did something to Nedra. You think I'm gonna let him get away with it?"

"He didn't do anything to her. You're wrong about that."

"The hell I am. Where is she, then?"

"Away on an extended vacation."

"You think I buy that crap?"

"She sent postcards to people telling them so."

"What people?"

"Friends, business associates."

"Let's see one of these cards."

"Not even if I had one with me."

"Then tell me where she's been all this time."

"You know I'm not going to do that."

"Why'd she go off so sudden? Why'd she shut down her business without telling anybody? Huh? You think I don't know about all that?"

"She had her reasons."

Cahill blew air through his nose, a sharp, wet sound. "Jerking my chain so I'll leave Runyon alone. Nice try, slick, but it won't work. He did something to Nedra, damn right he did— *that's* the truth."

"Why? Why would he harm her?"

"She blew him off, that's why. He told me so himself."

"He wouldn't hurt her for that. Or for any reason."

"I say different. He's so goddamn innocent, what's he doing hanging around her house all the time?"

"Keeping her affairs in order until she gets back."

"Bullshit. That don't make any sense. He's up to something."

"He's in love with her, can't leave her or her life alone. Hell, Cahill, if anybody ought to be able to understand that, it's you. Same reason you kept hassling her two years ago, why *you* started hanging around her place again as soon as you got out of Lompoc."

His eyes bored into me. Anger had flared in them, fusing with the malice; the combination was like a critical mass heating up, beginning to glow. You could feel the violence radiating off him. Unpredictable as a critical mass, too—liable to go off at any second. I moved my feet apart a little, shifted my weight forward, lifted my hands above waist level. If he exploded at me he was going to set off a second volatile pile that might just knock him on his ass.

"She got a restraining order against you once," I said. "She'll do it again when she comes home from her trip. You've got to know that."

Nothing from him.

"If Runyon doesn't put you back in the slam, if I don't, then Nedra will. Can't you see that? Don't you care whether or not they shut the door on you again?"

"I care," he said.

"Okay, then. Leave the Runyons alone and leave Nedra alone. No more phone calls, no more confrontations, no more threats, no more hassles. Walk away and start clean."

"Not if she's dead. Not if he made her that way."

"Then back off and let me handle it. I'll find her, prove she's alive, prove Runyon hasn't done anything to her."

"Why the hell should I?"

"I just told you why, for Christ's sake."

"You know what I say to that? I say fuck the Runyons. And fuck you, too, slick."

"If that's how you want to play it, fine. But hear this. You keep making trouble for them, you're going to have me and the cops to contend with. I don't push the way Runyon does. In fact I don't push at all."

"Big talk from an old fart."

"I can back it up."

"Sure you can. Break your neck with one little twist."

"Show me," I said.

He took a fast step toward me. It was a feint, to gauge my reaction; I didn't move, didn't flinch. I would have reacted the same way if it hadn't been a feint. A little time went by while we played stare-down. I could hear the wind in the vacant lot behind me, hear it rattling something nearby. Feel it cold against my skin.

"Well, Cahill?"

"That ain't gonna work with me either," he said.

"What isn't?"

"Push me into jumping you so you can hang another assault rap on me."

"I don't need to hang one on you. I told you, Runyon's prepared to do that himself after last night."

"You think I'm stupid? I'm not stupid. Runyon was gonna press charges, he'd already of done it and the cops'd be here rousting me, not you. He won't do it because he's afraid to, because of what he done to Nedra. I know that, even if you don't. You tell him I know. You tell him I'll find her one way or another, and when I do she better not be dead or hurt or he'll be the sorriest son of a bitch who ever lived."

"I'll take that as a threat on his life."

"Take it any damn way you want to."

Cahill hawked deep in his throat, spat a glob of mucus at my feet. When I still didn't move he gave me the meltdown stare again, then the crooked yellow grin like a door opening briefly under a furnace. Then he turned on his heel and stalked into the house and banged the door behind him.

Chapter **12**

MATT ANSWERED THE BELL at the Runyon house in Ashbury Heights. Giants sweatshirt today, sleeves cut off at the shoulders; in one hand he held a rumpled copy of the *Sporting News*. There was a thin line of blond fuzz on his upper lip, as if he'd suddenly decided to grow a mustache. He didn't seem happy to see me, but then he didn't seem unhappy either. The young-old eyes were as bleak as they'd been last night at S.F. General.

"How's it going?" I asked him.

"Shitty. You want to see my mom?"

"If she's home."

"Out back in her studio. I'll show you."

"How about your dad? Still in bed?"

"No, he's up."

"How's he feeling?"

"I don't know," Matt said.

"Not talking?"

Headshake. "I tried and Mom tried."

"He hasn't tried to leave the house?"

"No. Not yet."

He took me through the kitchen, out the back door. A covered walkway connected the house to an outbuilding that had been erected next to the garage. There was still plenty of yard—a long strip of lawn, flower beds, a liquidambar tree between the outbuilding and an eight-foot wooden fence with an access door shaped into it. Beyond the fence, partly visible from the porch, was one of the narrow pedestrian ladder streets that you find in some of the hillier sections of the city.

Matt knocked on the studio door and we went in. It was one big room, naturally lighted: the east wall and part of the ceiling were of glass. Ficus plants in redwood tubs gave it a partial greenhouse effect. But there was no mistaking the fact that it was a painter's studio. Canvases in various sizes were everywhere—finished, unfinished, blank; some displayed on easels and on the two white walls, others in rows along the floor. Kay Runyon, wearing a paint-spattered smock, stood before an easel set up in front of the glass wall, a table beside her cluttered with paints and brushes and an open bag of dryer lint. But she hadn't been working; just standing there, arms folded across her breasts, like a sculptured likeness of an artist in repose.

She turned abruptly as we entered. At first she seemed more pleased to see me than her son had been, but that didn't last long. One careful look at my face told her the news wasn't good; the hope died flickering. She made a gesture to Matt, who was hovering near the door, and he left us without a word. Then she picked up a rag, wet part of it from a tin of turpentine, and began to scrub at her hands—clean hands, no paint on them anywhere.

"You found out who he is," she said. "You saw him."

"Yes."

"And you couldn't frighten him or make him listen to reason."

"No, but I gave him plenty to think about."

"Is he as . . . dangerous as I think he is?"

I couldn't lie to her. "Potentially."

"I knew it. Tell me about him."

I told her. Cahill's name and where he lived, his prison

record, the restraining order two years ago, the gist of my conversation with him earlier. She listened stone-faced. When I was done she took cigarettes and a lighter from a pocket in her smock, set fire to a weed before she spoke.

"He'll come after Vic again." It wasn't a question.

"Not if I can talk your husband into filing an assault complaint against him."

"You can try," she said without much hope.

"Even if he won't do it," I said, "the situation with Cahill isn't as grim as it looks. He doesn't want to go back to prison. He knows he can't hurt your husband again without paying a high price; he's not anonymous any longer and neither are his motives. He's smart enough to realize that and I think it'll force him to put a leash on himself." I paused. "You know your husband far better than I do, Mrs. Runyon. Is he capable of violence against another human being?"

"My God," she said, "you don't think Cahill's right? That Vic did something to that woman?"

"I don't, no. I'm asking your opinion, if you think it's even remotely possible."

"No," she said. "Absolutely not."

"Then no matter how much Cahill might prod and threaten, there can't be anything for him to find, anything to set him off again. If I can find Nedra, alive or dead, and prove to Cahill that your husband is innocent, he'll take himself right out of your lives."

"If," she said. "That's a big *if.*"

"Maybe not. I've already turned up some leads." I told her about the postcards Dr. Muncon had received.

"That proves Nedra is alive, doesn't it?"

"Not to Cahill; he didn't believe me when I told him about the cards. I'm not so sure I buy it either."

"You doubt that she sent them?"

"Muncon said they were in her handwriting and handwriting isn't as easy to fake as people think. What bothers me is that Muncon received cards but your husband apparently didn't; and

I've yet to find any evidence that she sent cards or letters to any of her clients. Why only to her therapist? Something doesn't ring true.''

"Yes, I see what you mean.'' She jabbed out her cigarette in an oyster shell ashtray, immediately lit another. "Even if you do find her, it'll take time. Won't it? A lot of time?''

"It might. Then again, I might get lucky.''

"What do we do in the meantime?''

"About Cahill? Unless your husband presses assault charges, I'm afraid there's nothing much you can do. Except to not provoke him if he calls again. And first thing Monday, contact the phone company and have your number changed.''

"What if he comes here to the house?''

"I don't think he will.''

"But if he does?''

"Don't let him in, don't talk to him under any circumstances. But the best safeguard is not to be here, none of you.''

"You mean convince Vic to go away for a while.''

"The three of you, yes. Visit friends . . . go someplace you've enjoyed together in the past, familiar surroundings.''

"He won't do that either,'' she said. "I can't get him to do *anything* anymore. He just won't listen to me.''

"Is he talking to you at all?''

"Barely.''

"Say anything about what happened with Cahill?''

"Not a word. He's in a great deal of pain. I think if he wasn't he'd have tried to leave, to go back to her house today. I hid his car keys, both sets. Ridiculous, isn't it? Having to do a thing like that with a forty-year-old man?''

I put an awkward hand on her arm. Gently I said, "Maybe I can get through to him. He was willing enough to talk to me on the way to the hospital.''

"To a stranger but not to his wife and son.''

"Guilt, Mrs. Runyon. You know that.''

"Yes, I know, but it still hurts. . . .'' Angrily she snuffed out her second cancer stick. "Oh, shit,'' she said, "let's go inside. I don't know why I came out here in the first place. I thought painting might ease my mind, but I should have known better. I can't concentrate—I can barely think straight.''

Inside the house, in the kitchen, she said, ''Would you like a drink? Some coffee?''

''No, thanks.''

''I'm going to have a Scotch. I need one. You want to talk to Vic alone, don't you?''

''It would be better that way.''

''He's in the TV room. At least, that's where he was earlier. Straight through that door over there.''

I went through the door and across a dining area, following the muted babble of television voices. The TV room was large, comfortably furnished. No Dreamsicle effect here; the color scheme was autumnal browns and golds. Victor Runyon sat in a recliner, both feet flat on the floor. He wore slippers and a bathrobe. The bandage across the middle of his face, the bruises that had spread upward from his broken nose to darken his eyes, made him look grotesque and pathetic. I might have felt compassion for him if he'd been a different sort of man, suffering for different reasons; as it was, I felt nothing. All my tender mercies were reserved for his wife and son.

The pained eyes stared blankly at a twenty-five-inch TV screen, where cartoon characters screeched and gabbled and chased each other across a cartoon landscape. He didn't know I was there until I moved over to form a block between him and the screen; then he blinked and his head lifted and he stared at me.

''Remember me?'' I said. ''I'm the detective who hauled your sorry ass to the hospital last night.''

That failed to get a rise out of him. He said in a monotone, ''I remember.''

''I've identified the man who attacked you. His name is Cahill, Eddie Cahill. He's been in prison twice before, once for felony assault. Two years ago, before he went to jail the second time, he threatened and harassed Nedra Merchant to the point where she had a lawyer obtain a restraining order against him. She never told you about that?''

''No.''

''He's a dangerous man, Runyon. A threat to you and your family. Something has to be done about him.''

No answer.

''I'm telling you the hard truth here. I saw him again this afternoon, tried to talk sense to him; he won't listen. He's convinced you've harmed Nedra in some way. Sooner or later he'll come after you, or maybe after your wife and son. You can prevent that by pressing assault charges against him. How about it, Runyon?''

''Go to the police? Tell them about Nedra and me?''

''Yes.''

''I can't,'' he said.

''Why not? A lot of people know the truth now—your wife, your son, me, Cahill, Nedra's ex-husband, her shrink, a couple of others. What difference does it make if the police know too?''

Silence.

''If you don't give a damn about yourself, fine. But think about your family for a change.''

''I won't let anything happen to my family.''

''No? How are you going to prevent it?''

''I won't let anything happen.''

''There's Nedra too,'' I said. ''He'll be a threat to her when she comes home, if you don't put him back in prison where he belongs.''

''Nedra,'' Runyon said. As if he were invoking the name of a deity.

''So? What's it going to be?''

''I have to think.''

''Don't take too long.''

''I won't.'' He moved painfully in the chair. ''Go away now, will you? Leave me alone.''

''One question first,'' I said, and asked him about the empty spare-key hook in Nedra's desk drawer, the one marked "Thorn." "Mean anything to you—the abbreviation?"

"No."

"You're sure? There's no place she used to go that starts with 'Thorn.,' no person she knows with that kind of name?"

"No," he said again, and again he shifted position, wincing. "Please go away. Talking makes my face hurt."

Mine, too—talking to him. I went away and left him alone.

KERRY HADN'T CALLED BACK. The only message on my office machine was from James Keverne, Nedra Merchant's attorney.

I sat down at my desk. After six-thirty now; the building was silent as a tomb. Too late to call Keverne back—but he would be in his office tomorrow morning, he'd said. Too late to do much of anything else work-related tonight. The evening stretched out ahead, so long and far that I couldn't see the end of it. Friday evening. For most people it was T.G.I.F., the beginning of a weekend of freedom. Dinners out, shows, nightclubs, ball games . . . lovemaking too. But not for me. Not for Kerry, either, by her own testimony.

Why hadn't she called back? She couldn't be *that* busy, for Christ's sake.

I caught up the phone, punched out her private number at Bates and Carpenter. No answer. *Not tonight. I just can't. I've got to get some more work done on the Blessing account.* I stayed on the line, and pretty soon the call was switched automatically to B and C's in-house switchboard. I asked the operator if Kerry was still on the premises; she said Ms. Wade was unavailable. What the hell did that mean, unavailable? It sounded evasive. I asked when Ms. Wade would be available and the operator said she didn't know, did I want to leave a message? No, I said, no message.

I went and got some water and put it on the hot plate to boil. Then I watched it boil. Then I made a cup of instant coffee. Things to do with my hands and my eyes; little time killers.

Getting darker in here now, even though there were still a couple of hours of daylight left: clouds crawling over the sky, fat gray bloated things that shut out the sun. The night sounds were already starting—groans and mutters in the walls, like an old man complaining aloud to himself. Why don't buildings make noises in the daytime? Or if they do, why don't we hear them even when it's quiet? Why do old joints creak and phantoms walk only at night?

I took my coffee to the desk. And in my mind's eye I could see myself sitting there in the darkening room, hunched and alone with the cup steaming in one hand. Pathetic image, like one of those black-and-white studies you see in arty photographic books, above titles like "Estranged" and "Study in Twilight."

To hell with that; no man wants to view himself as a cliché. I got up again, carried the coffee down the hall to the toilet, and emptied it out. Then I locked up and let the spooks have the office and the building to themselves.

Chapter **13**

THE HEAVY FRIDAY NIGHT EXODUS from the city had eased somewhat, so traffic on the Golden Gate Bridge was no longer a stop-
and-go snarl. I drove across and then down into Sausalito. Parking along the main drag, Bridgeway, was out of the question, but
I lucked into a space on one of the hillside streets not too far
away. Standing-room-only at the No-Name Bar, where I went
sometimes when I wanted a gaggle of people around me and
where I had once met Sterling Hayden, the actor and writer. I had
two beers and didn't talk to anyone on this visit except a waitress, who looked right through me. I was there fifteen minutes; it
was as if I weren't there at all. A lot of imaginative types think it
would be amusing to have the power of invisibility, even for just
a day, like the character in the H. G. Wells story. I know it
wouldn't be.

Bayfront and other downtown restaurants were all packed,
with waiting lists of an hour or more. I drove out to the north part
of town, where there are some little eating places in shopping
centers, and found one where I had to wait only ten minutes for a
table. I splurged on a crab Louie and another beer. Didn't talk to

anybody there either; the waiter paid no more attention to me as an individual than the No-Name waitress.

Afterward I went for a walk along the bay. The way the dark water moved, the way the lights shimmered on the surface, as though they were trapped beneath it rather than reflected off it, had an oddly hypnotic effect on me. I could feel the pull of all that quiet, rippling dark, the allure of it . . . and after a while it made me uneasy. This was no place for me tonight, feeling as I did, with the loneliness and the uncertainty about Kerry weighing heavy on my mind. No damn place for a loner to be alone.

Back to the car, back to the city. I knew where I was going without having to think about it.

THE BUILDING IN WHICH Bates and Carpenter had its offices was a high-rise on Kearney, on the fringe of the Financial District. The doors were locked at six o'clock on weeknights, so you had to go through the security desk to get in or out afterhours. For nonemployees of one of the firms, that meant you couldn't get past the lobby without authorization and proper ID. And employees and nonemployees alike had to sign in and out.

I rang the lobby bell and the guard on the desk came over to see what I wanted. His name was Ben Spicer; I knew him because he was a retired cop, like a lot of night security people, and because I'd been here after six to meet Kerry on several occasions. He opened up as soon as he recognized me.

"Kerry Wade still working late at B and C, Ben?"

"No, you missed her. She left a couple of hours ago."

". . . That long? You sure?"

"Positive."

"Alone?"

"Somebody with her, I think. At least they signed out at the same time."

"Man or woman?"

"Man."

"Tall, slender, good-looking, silver at the temples?"

"That's him."

Metallic taste in my mouth now. "You know who he is?"

"Well, he doesn't work for B and C or anyplace else in the building, I can tell you that. But I've seen him before."

"With Kerry, recently?"

"Time or two, now that I think about it," Spicer said. "Why? You got a problem?"

I made myself smile; it felt like a rictus. "No, no problem. What's his name, Ben?"

"I'm lousy with names of people I don't know. I can check the register."

"If you wouldn't mind."

He crossed to the security desk, consulted the register, came back. "Paul Blessing. Odd name. Count your blessings, huh?"

"Yeah," I said. *I've* got *to do some more work on the Blessing account.* Or on Paul Blessing himself. Count your blessings. "Kerry didn't happen to say where she was going, did she?"

"Afraid she didn't."

"Thanks, Ben."

"Sure. Hope everything's okay. You look kind of sick."

"Something I ate, that's all."

Double lie. Something I was trying to swallow and couldn't choke down.

IN THE DAYS BEFORE HIV began killing people, Henry the Eighth's had been a flagship in the sexual revolution—a singles hangout, a meat market. Kerry had told me that once and I'd kidded her about having firsthand knowledge. She'd been mildly offended. Casual sex wasn't for her; never had been, never would be. She had to care about a man before she went to bed with him. "Contrary to what you may think," she'd said, "I am not an easy lay."

Count your blessings.

These days, with AIDS a full-scale epidemic thanks to head-in-the-sand politicians, Henry the Eighth's had a new, more sedate image. Live jazz had replaced canned rock, and sex was no longer the primary topic of conversation. Men took their wives there now. Men took their lady friends and mistresses there too. Men like Barney Rivera. Men like Paul Blessing.

Not tonight, though. Big Friday night crowd, dancing, drinking, couples holding hands and intimate discussions; it took me a while to canvass the place, hating what I was doing the whole time. Hating myself, too, because now I wasn't just the sad loner, the invisible man, but a different and even more piteous cliché: man on the hunt for a woman who might be cheating. The kind of job I despised when it was offered to me professionally. The kind of job, in reverse, that Joe DeFalco had talked me into doing for Kay Runyon.

Kerry wasn't there. I saw a couple of tall, fortyish, silver-templed types, but the women they were with were strangers. Been here and gone? Where? His place? Hers? Would she take him home with her? Bad enough if she went with him, but if she took him to her apartment, if she took him into the bed she'd shared with me . . .

SHE HADN'T. Not tonight anyway.

I drove from the Financial District to Diamond Heights, hating myself even more, and made two passes in front of her building on Gold Mine Drive. No sign of her car. Then I dropped down to the street below, parked and got out at a point where you could look up and see her balcony and windows. The drapes were drawn and the lights were off.

PAUL BLESSING.

All right, who *was* Paul Blessing?

Back downtown, driving in a kind of fog now. O'Farrell again, and into my building, and upstairs to my office. Telephone directory. Blessing, Paul or P. No listing. But there was a listing for Blessing Furniture Showrooms on Mission and Sixteenth. The Yellow Pages carried a half-page ad for Blessing Furniture Showrooms; they specialized in solid oak and walnut furnishings and sofa beds, and had three branches—Cupertino, Lafayette, and Millbrae. Large enough operation to benefit from a professionally orchestrated advertising campaign. And Bates and Carpenter actively solicited the business of small chain outfits in a variety of enterprises.

I hauled out my accumulation of White Pages for the nine Bay Area counties and began to hunt through them. He lived in Marin County; at least, there was a listing for Blessing, Paul M., in Tiburon, and Tiburon was the kind of upscale community that attracted successful business types. I copied down the address and telephone number. Then I combed the remaining directories to find out if there were any other Paul or P. Blessings in the area. There weren't.

I wondered if he had a wife over there in Tiburon.

I wondered if he and Kerry were in a motel room somewhere.

I wondered if he loved her or was just using her.

I wondered if she loved him.

After a while, when I was sick with wondering, I closed up the office again and went home to wonder some more.

I KEPT THINKING, sitting in the dark of my living room, that it was my fault.

That in a way I had set it up—not the specific circumstances of the affair, but the climate that had allowed it to happen. Unconsciously, but with the same precision and results as if it had been a calculated plan. Loner, workaholic, lapsed idealist . . . that was me, all right. But no matter what I had led myself to believe, Kerry was none of those things. She needed people; she needed a well-rounded life; she needed dreams and ideals to sustain her. And from me she needed more than a few hours or a few days, catch-as-catch-can—uninspired, predictable hours and days at that, with no excitement and no real passion except in bed. All my careful rationalizations about how much alike we were were so much crap. Soulmates? No way. Her soul was bright and mine was dark—and it was possible, even probable, that she'd understood that longer and better than I did, that it was the one true reason she refused to marry me.

My fault. Sad-eyed loner with his heart on his sleeve . . .
not such a bad way to look at yourself, because it was an accept-
able self-image. The troubled knight, good and noble, jousting
for justice. But in others' eyes, the image might not be half so
appealing. What was my kind of loner, when you broke him
down to basics, but a weak and selfish person? Pretending other
people matter a great deal to him, paying lip service to how
much empathy he has—but maybe the truth is, no one matters
much except as they pertain directly to him, and his only real
empathy is for himself.

The few individuals he lets get close to him are there to feed
his vanity, to help him maintain his positive self-image. Ah, but
those few have minds of their own, different needs and agendas,
different ways of looking at things, and sooner or later they begin
to chafe under the yoke of his selfishness, to stop collaborating in
it. And instead of understanding, adapting, he shifts the blame to
them and maneuvers them out of his life.

Eberhardt . . . was that the way it was with him? He'd
wanted his freedom, he said—from me, from my way of doing
things. From years of being folded and stuffed into neat little
slots that conformed with my view of what he was and ought to
be? From an egotistical tyrant who was so well insulated he
didn't even know he was either one? No wonder he'd quit me.

No wonder Kerry might be quitting me.

And when they were both gone, the seal would be complete.
I'd become a self-fulfilled prophecy: the true dark-souled loner,
forever lost inside himself, shrieking his pain in a wilderness
where no one was left to hear or care.

I WENT TO BED expecting to sleep little, and to have bad
dreams when I did drop off. Instead I went out as soon as I went
down, and stayed out until gray dawn, and didn't dream at all.
But it was not a good rest. I awoke feeling logy, with grit in my
eyes and a tightness behind them, like the residue of a severe
migraine. Not even a long, hot shower and three cups of coffee
took away much of the grinding tiredness.

At least I didn't feel as bad about myself this morning. You never hate anyone as much in the daylight as you do in the dark, including the party that stares back at you from the bathroom mirror. Weak, selfish, egotistical tyrant? Dark-souled loner? All of those things in a way, yes, but none to any radical degree. Nor was what had happened with Eberhardt, what was happening with Kerry, all my fault. It takes two to screw up a personal relationship, no matter what the circumstances. I'd be a hell of a lot better able to cope with what lay ahead if I kept that in mind.

Another thing, too: Nobody can screw up a man's relationship with himself worse than he can, working alone.

Chapter **14**

"HELLO?" Woman's voice, not young, not old, with a faint trace of an accent.

"Is this the Blessing residence?"

"Yes, it is."

"The Paul Blessing who owns Blessing's Furniture Showrooms?"

"That's right. You want to talk to Mr. Blessing?"

What would I say to him? Good morning, I'm Kerry Wade's significant other and I'd like to know if you're screwing her and how serious things are between the two of you in any case. Oh, and by the way, was that your wife I just spoke to?

"Hello?" the woman said. "You still there?"

"I'm here."

"Okay, I'll get him for you—"

"No, that's not necessary. Are you Mrs. Blessing?"

"What?"

"Mrs. Blessing, Paul's wife."

"Me?" She made a noise that was either a snort or a laugh. "I'm the housekeeper."

"Is Mrs. Blessing home?"

"There isn't a Mrs. Blessing. No more."

"Oh? Divorce?"

"She died," the woman said. "Last year."

I couldn't think of anything to say to that.

"I have work to do," she said. "What's your name? I'll tell Mr. Blessing and you talk to him—"

"Thanks, but don't disturb him. I'll call again later."

I hung up feeling like a fool. So now I knew the Paul Blessing in Tiburon was the right one and that he was a widower. So what? What was I going to do with the knowledge? Confront him —get in his face, tell him to leave Kerry alone? Threaten him, pound on him . . . the Mr. Macho, Eddie Cahill approach? For Christ's sake, I had no claims on Kerry, and Blessing was as legally unattached as she was, and we were all adults here anyway, right? These things happened and you had to accept them, bow out gracefully if it came to that, *que será, será.* That was the only civilized way to deal with it, the only intelligent way. Even if you were hurting and scared right down to the marrow.

Damn office was cold, even though I'd put the heat on when I came in. Fog capered outside the skylights, running and tumbling under the lash of an icy ocean wind. The wind would banish the fog later on and there'd be sun most of the day, but right now there was the cold and the gray. I got up and put my overcoat back on and sat down again. And stared at the phone. And picked up the receiver and tapped out Kerry's number.

Click, and a humming, and: "Hello. I can't come to the phone right now, but if you'll leave your name and number I'll return your call as soon as—"

I banged the receiver down, the first time I had ever disconnected without talking to her machine. There wasn't any point in leaving a message. She knew I wanted to see her, and the fact that she hadn't called meant she was avoiding me. Guilt, fear, whatever.

I stared at the phone some more. God, I wished there was somebody I could talk to about this. Cybil? Kerry wouldn't have told her mother she was having an affair. Cybil was back on my side after months of shunning me; and Kerry wouldn't have wanted to upset her now that she had finally recovered from the year-long depression caused by her husband Ivan's sudden death. And if I broke the news to Cybil, it would do more harm than good. I did not want to burden her any more than Kerry did.

Bobbie Jean? She and Kerry were still friends, but I doubted that Kerry would confide in her about a thing like this. I couldn't either. I had spoken to Bobbie Jean only once since Eberhardt walked out, right afterward; she'd called to say how sorry she was. It had been an awkward conversation, and a brief one. She was too tightly linked to Eberhardt for us to go on being comfortable with each other, and we both knew it.

Who else was there? Nobody else. Not Barney Rivera, that little prick; the way I felt now I would never deal with him again, personally or professionally. Not Joe DeFalco. Not any of my other acquaintances.

Kerry was the only one.

Well, she wouldn't hide out for long; she wasn't made that way. Still, I was not going to just hang and rattle. Better for both of us if it came from her, straight out, so I'd give her the weekend—no more. If she was still avoiding me come Monday, I'd force it. Any longer than that and I might not be emotionally capable of handling it the right way.

One more call, business this time, then I'd get out of here, get some people around me. Worst place for me right now was alone in a room, any room.

Annette Olroyd's number. Four rings, and an elderly female voice said formally, "Yes? May I help you?"

"Ms. Olroyd?"

"No, this is her mother. Annette is out of town just now."

"When do you expect her back?"

"Sometime this evening. May I take a message?"

"Yes, please." I gave my name and profession. "Tell your daughter I'd like to talk to her on an urgent matter concerning Nedra Merchant."

"Oh. She isn't in any trouble, is she?"

"Your daughter? No, not at all—"

"I meant Nedra. Annette will be terribly upset if she is."

"Do you know Nedra, Mrs. . . . ?"

"Mrs. Davis. I don't know her well, but I met her once and liked her."

"Is she a close friend of Annette's?"

"Not close, no. She was a godsend."

"How do you mean?"

"Well . . . her counsel helped Annette through a very difficult time, you know." Mrs. Davis seemed to think I had some knowledge of the relationship between her daughter and Nedra Merchant; that was one reason she was being open with me. Another was that she was probably the chatty, unassuming type. "Much more so than Dr. Muncon's, I must say."

"Dr. Philip Muncon?"

"Yes, that's right. Do you know him?"

"We've met. Is that how your daughter met Nedra, through the doctor?"

"At his office, yes. She was so devastated when Bob left her, it seemed that therapy was the only solution. We didn't dream that another of his patients would be the one to provide it."

Right. Who knew men and how to deal with the breakup of a male-female relationship better than a woman like Nedra Merchant? She must have taken pity on Annette Olroyd. She may not have had any women friends—may not have liked women much, as her ex-husband had testified—but the role of sage and mother confessor is difficult for anyone to resist.

I asked, "How long has it been since Annette last saw Nedra?"

"Oh, several months," Mrs. Davis said. "Nedra left the city suddenly, you know."

"Yes. I'm trying to locate her."

"Annette was upset at first; she thought something might

have happened to Nedra. You can imagine how relieved she was when she found out that wasn't the case.''

"How did she find it out?"

"Nedra wrote to her."

"Wrote to her. A postcard, by any chance?"

"Yes, that's right."

"More than one?"

"Two, I believe."

"Can you tell me where the cards were mailed?"

"A resort area . . . a lake somewhere. I don't recall which one."

"Lake Tahoe?"

"No, I don't think it was Lake Tahoe."

"Did you see any of the cards, Mrs. Davis?"

"No, I'm sorry, I didn't."

"Did Annette tell you what they said?"

"Oh, you know, the usual things people write on postcards. She was fine and expected to be away for quite a while."

"Would you know if your daughter saved the cards?"

"I expect she did. Annette inherited my packrat tendencies."

"Would you be able to find them?"

". . . You mean now? Without Annette's permission?"

"Yes, ma'am. I wouldn't ask except that it's very important I locate Nedra as soon as possible. The name of the lake and the town or towns where they were mailed would be a great help."

"Oh, I couldn't. I don't have any idea where she might have put them and I don't believe in invading *anyone's* privacy, even in a good cause. No, I'm sorry, but I think it's best if you talk to Annette about this when she gets back."

JAMES KEVERNE was what the newspeak advocates would call "a person of weight." He stood about five-nine, would probably tip the scales at 275, and had two well-defined chins and an incipient third. He also had male-pattern baldness—what hair he still owned was carrot-colored and curly—and a none too jovial manner. Nedra Merchant's relationship with him, I thought as we shook hands, figured to be strictly professional.

I told him I was investigating a matter involving Nedra Merchant; that she'd dropped out of sight under unusual circumstances in early May and I was trying to find her. He said he hadn't had any dealings with her in over a year. He also said he knew virtually nothing about her private life. I believed him on both counts.

He asked then, "Do you suspect foul play?"

"It's a possibility."

"Is that the reason you're here? My paralegal said you mentioned a restraining order. The one I obtained against Edward Cahill, I assume."

"That's right."

"You think Cahill is involved in her disappearance?"

"No," I said. "He was still in prison in May; he got out just three weeks ago."

"I knew he'd been sent back to prison, of course," Keverne said. "A felony assault charge, wasn't it? Ms. Merchant was very relieved."

"He made life pretty miserable for her, I understand."

"Yes. She was terrified of him."

"Well, I'm afraid prison didn't straighten him out any. He's still obsessed with her. He's been hanging around her house, and two nights ago he committed another assault, against a friend of hers. He also has been making threatening telephone calls to the friend and the friend's family."

"I see."

"If Nedra Merchant is alive and well, and he finds out where she is, he'll make trouble for her again. Unless he can be put back behind bars."

"Naturally I'd like to help put him there. And help you find Ms. Merchant. But I don't see how I can do either."

"Neither do I. Frankly, Mr. Keverne, I'm grabbing at straws."

"About all I can tell you are the details of Cahill's harassment two years ago, if you'd care to hear them."

"I would, yes."

Keverne folded his hands together; they were thick-fingered and as red as a washerwoman's. "Cahill made dozens of telephone calls to Ms. Merchant. At first they were pleading, cajoling; all he wanted, he said, was to spend some time with her. Inevitably they turned sexual in nature, and finally threatening."

"Did she change her telephone number?"

"Of course. Under the circumstances, it did no good."

"What circumstances?"

"Cahill had been fired by then, but he still had access to telephone company records. I suppose a fellow employee helped him."

"Wait a minute. Cahill worked for Pac Bell?"

"You didn't know that?"

"No, I didn't. In what capacity?"

"Repairman and installer," Keverne said. "Ms. Merchant was having a problem with one of her extension phones and Cahill was the man sent out to fix it. She made the mistake of being nice to him and he misinterpreted her motives. The calls began the next day."

I asked Keverne a few more questions—about the incidents in which Cahill had accosted Nedra Merchant in public, mainly. But they were in the interest of thoroughness; the answers were irrelevant. My mind was on what he'd already told me, forming a hunch that grew stronger by the minute.

If the hunch proved out, Eddie Cahill was even more slyly dangerous than I'd thought. And James Keverne might just have handed me the key to lock him away inside another prison cell.

IN MY CAR I used the mobile phone to call George Agonistes at his home in San Bruno. He was a fellow private investigator, one of the new breed of specialist; we'd once worked on the same job, from different angles, and developed a mutual respect for each other's abilities. We exchanged favors every now and then, ours being a back-scratching kind of business.

He was home and he wanted to stay there. "I don't work Saturdays or Sundays," he said, "not for any amount of money."

"I think I can get my client to pay five hundred for an afternoon's work."

"Maybe I could make an exception," he said.

I gave him the Crestmont address, asked how long before he could meet me there. He said twelve-thirty. It was eleven now. An hour and a half was plenty of time for me to swing by Ashbury Heights on the way.

"Twelve-thirty's fine. Bring all your equipment, George. I don't know what kind of thing we're dealing with here."

"You insult my professionalism," Agonistes said. "I never go out on a job without a full load. Not these days, I don't."

KAY RUNYON OPENED THE DOOR to my ring, custard-pale, squinting through the smoke from one of her cigarettes. She started to speak, but I put my finger to my lips and caught her arm and drew her out onto the porch. Then I motioned for her to shut the door, to follow me down to the landing between the two flights of brick steps.

"What is it?" she said then. "What's going on?"

"I didn't want to talk in the house."

"Vic's lying down, he wouldn't have heard us—"

"It's not Vic I'm worried about."

"I don't understand. . . ."

"Have you had any maintenance or repair people here in the past three weeks? A man from the telephone company who showed up without being called?"

She said blankly, "The phone company?"

"Wanting to check a line or phone inside."

". . . A repairman did come out, yes, but—"

"Describe him."

"I wasn't here."

"Who was? Matt?"

"Yes. He mentioned it when I came home that night."

"Is Matt here now?"

She nodded.

"Go in and ask him to come out here with you. Don't say anything else."

"Will you please tell me what's going on—?"

"Go get Matt. Then I'll tell both of you."

She hurried into the house, returned with her son in tow. I said to him, "Your mother tells me a man from the telephone company showed up a while back."

"Yeah. A repair guy."

"When was that?"

"I don't know, a couple of weeks ago."

"What did he tell you?"

"He said there was a problem with the lines in the neighborhood and he needed to check our phones. He told me what it was, the problem, but it didn't mean anything to me."

"And you let him inside?"

"Well, I didn't see any reason not to. I mean, he was wearing a uniform and a tool belt with all the junk phone repair guys carry, and he showed me an ID card with his picture on it."

"What name was on the ID card?"

"I didn't pay much attention."

"How long was he in the house?"

"Half an hour or so."

"Were you with him the whole time?"

"I don't remember. . . . I guess not, no."

"Describe him for me, Matt."

"He was . . . I don't know, short, about my folks' age. Built pretty good—like he worked out a lot."

"Losing his hair? Reddish face?"

"Yeah, that's right. What—?"

Kay Runyon made a sharp little noise in her throat. "My God, it was Cahill, wasn't it?"

"I'm afraid so." Wearing his old uniform and tool belt,

flashing his old Pac Bell ID—all kept illegally after he was fired
and then stashed somewhere while he was in prison. At his sister's home, probably.

"What was he doing *here*?"

"I think he was planting bugs," I said.

"Bugs?"

Matt knew; seventeen-year-old kids know a hell of a lot
more these days than my generation did at that age. "Listening
devices," he said angrily. The anger was directed at himself as
much as at Eddie Cahill. "He put them in the house so he could
spy on us. And it's my damn fault, I let him in so he could do
it."

I told him it wasn't his fault, but he didn't want to hear that.
He smacked his thigh with a closed fist, several times, hard, as if
he were inflicting corporal punishment on himself.

"Listening to us?" Kay Runyon said. She was staring at
me. "Everything we said and did in this house for the past two
weeks?"

"Not everything, no. Random eavesdropping, just enough
to frustrate him. The only thing he found out was that you hired
me."

"A man like that, a violent criminal? How could he have
the technical knowledge . . . ?"

"He once worked for the telephone company," I said, "and
he once worked for a microelectronics firm. And you don't need
to be an expert to make and install a listening device. You can
buy the components at Radio Shack and learn how to put them
together from a book you can special-order at Crown or B. Dal-
ton."

"My God."

"The important thing is that if he did bug your house, he
committed a felony that'll put him right back in prison. Matt can
identify him positively; press charges for illegal trespass and
eavesdropping and they'll stick. With his record, his background,
your testimony and mine, it should be enough to get a conviction
even if your husband remains silent."

"How soon can we have him arrested?"

"Charges can be filed as soon as we have proof of the bugging."

"How long will that take?"

"Not long. A few hours."

"Those . . . things can be found that quickly? Gotten rid of?"

"Yes. I know an exterminator; I'll go see him now, try to get him here by three o'clock at the latest."

The hope in Kay Runyon's eyes was thin and wary; too much painful disillusionment had made her emotionally gun-shy. She said, "Should I tell Vic?"

"No. I'll do that when I come back. While you're waiting, don't say anything about the bugs or Cahill; the transmitters could be anywhere. If you want to talk, stick to normal topics."

"Normal topics," she said. "There's nothing normal in our lives anymore. I wonder if there ever will be again."

Matt put his arm around her shoulders; she leaned against him. I left them there like that and went to meet George Agonistes, the electronic surveillance industry's version of the Orkin man.

Chapter 15

AGONISTES WAS WAITING in his light-blue van when I got up to Crestmont. The van didn't look like much from the outside, but behind its smoke-tinted windows was some of the most sophisticated electronics equipment available—everything from laser shotguns to spike mikes to microtransmitters no larger than a pea. All sorts of debuggers, too, that being his particular specialty, including a thing he'd shown me once called a nonlinear junction detector that looked like nothing so much as a vacuum cleaner and was used to uncover body bugs and wired briefcases, to find concealed listening devices by scanning radios, tape recorders, TV sets, and the like. None of it made a whole lot of sense to me from the technological standpoint, but then it didn't have to. I had my end of the detecting business and Agonistes had his, and the twain had no interest in meeting except on rare occasions like this one.

I parked behind his van, climbed out. This being Saturday, the neighborhood wasn't as quiet or deserted as it was on weekdays: couple of kids on skateboards, a woman working in her front yard, a man washing his car. Homey activities; day-off pleasures. I envied the adults . . . now more than ever. Theirs was a world I could only observe from the outside, as if through a thick pane of glass. Men like me don't have weekend lives. For us, every day is Monday, and too often a blue Monday at that—

Bullshit, I thought.

More of the self-indulgent loner crap. I could be one of those Mr. Averages if I wanted it badly enough. Anybody can change; you just need the proper incentive. Maybe if I'd tried harder to integrate myself into the mainstream of society, Kerry and I wouldn't have come to the big crisis point we were at now.

Agonistes seemed to be in no hurry to quit his van, so I went around to the passenger side and opened the door and slid in next to him. I hadn't seen him in ten months, but he wouldn't have changed much if it had been ten years. He still reminded me of a shrub that needed pruning. Thin, brown, gnarly body, topped by a wild tangle of bristly hair like an Afro that had gone to seed. But under that thatch was a mind as sensitive and finely tuned as one of the pieces of equipment he worked with.

"Been waiting long?"

"Few minutes," he said. "Nice neighborhood. Never been up here before."

"Country living in an urban environment."

"What do you suppose one of these houses costs?"

"More than you or I could ever afford." Especially him. He made a good living, but he had a wife and four kids—and his electronics mistress cost him as much to support as his family.

"Sad but true," he said. "Neighborhood-watch program here, I'll bet. See that woman up the street? She's already noticed us sitting here. Not a good area to set up a lengthy street surveillance."

"Nope."

"Your wiseguy live around here?" he asked. "Wiseguy" was Agonistes's generic term for anyone, male or female, professional or amateur, law officer or felon, who indulged in electronic surveillance.

"No. In Daly City."

"Probably not simple room bugs then. They send out radio signals on a standard eighty-eight to one-oh-eight megahertz FM band, but they don't have much range. Half a mile, max, with a relay transmitter."

"Uh-huh."

"He could've hidden a voice-actuated recorder somewhere within range, but that's not too likely, not in a neighborhood like this."

"Uh-huh."

"Probably not carrier current bugs either. You know what they are?"

"No."

"Wiseguys put them in the electrical system, inside a wall outlet," Agonistes said. "Then when they want to tune in, they use a radio somewhere in private, like their own homes. You get hiss and crackle with bugs like that, sometimes too much, and they amplify room noise; I don't like 'em. You said your wiseguy worked for the phone company?"

"Two years ago. I think that's when he planted the bugs in the house across the street. But a simple phone tap doesn't have any range either, right?"

"Right. A standard phone tap also doesn't have a long life."

"What does?"

"Infinity transmitter."

"Uh-huh."

"A nasty little mother," Agonistes said. "Works off a room's telephone or electrical current. Endless supply of power —transmission to infinity, theoretically. See?"

"I see."

"They're small, about a quarter-inch in diameter, so you can stick them any damn place—telephones, under carpets and furniture, behind electrical outlet switch plates. You can even hard-wire them into walls and cover them with conductive paint, then over that with regular paint. Conductive paint carries electricity the same as copper wires."

"How do they work?"

"Tone-activated. Wiseguy calls his target's number and blows a whistle into the receiver as soon as he hears the ring. Whistle shorts out the ring and activates the I.T."

"And then he can listen in as long as he wants, on his own telephone?"

"Right," Agonistes said. "Or from any telephone from here to Zimbabwe. If anybody else calls the target while the wiseguy's listening, the party gets a busy signal."

"And if the target happens to pick up his phone?"

"Dead or hissing line."

"Bugs like that must not be too easy to track down."

"On the contrary. All you need is an R.F. detector. R.F.—radio frequency."

"Which you've got."

"Which I've got."

"Can you deactivate I.T.s without removing them?"

"Sure. Is that what you want?"

"For now."

"Why?"

"It's a tricky situation." I explained it to him, in detail. When I was done, his thin lips had a sour, downward pull.

"So what we're talking about here," he said, "is one of the same felonies the wiseguy pulled. Illegal trespass."

"Technically, yes. Morally, no. You have a problem with that?"

"Not if it doesn't put my ass in a sling. I got mouths to feed."

"It won't," I said. "If Nedra Merchant is alive and well, she'll thank us for this and authorize you to pull the bugs. Pay you extra for it, too, probably."

"Suppose she's not alive and well?"

"Then it's a moot point. Her only relative is an elderly aunt in Texas and the aunt's not likely to complain about illegal trespass in a good cause even if she finds out about it. Which she won't."

Agonistes sighed. "Let's get it done."

He opened up the back of the van and removed a tool kit and his R.F. detector, an instrument about the size and outward appearance of a small black leather suitcase. The woman up the street glanced our way as we crossed to Nedra Merchant's house, but she wasn't curious enough or suspicious enough to come down and ask questions. We moved and acted casually, as if we belonged there.

When we were through the gate, Agonistes said, "No talking once we're inside. Nearest phone first. Kitchen? Living room?"

"Kitchen and family room."

"Kitchen, then."

I keyed us in. On the drainboard in the kitchen, Agonistes opened the R.F. detector to reveal a radarlike screen, meters, a set of headphones. He did some fiddling with the equipment, put the headphones on, did some more fiddling. Then he picked up the detector and approached the wall phone, and as soon as he did that the screen and meter needles began to dance. I figured that he was also hearing some kind of tone through the earphones, one that coordinated with the visual register on the screen. The louder the tone, the closer the bug.

There was one behind the plate for the phone jack; he found it in thirty seconds flat, showed it to me when he had the plate off. It looked innocent enough, about the size and shape of a square sugar cube. He did something to deactivate it, replaced the wall plate, and we moved on to the family room.

He found an I.T. in there, too, inside the phone itself. And another in the wall thermostat in the downstairs hallway, halfway between Nedra Merchant's bedroom and office; that bug evidently drew its power from the wires serving the thermostat. There were two bugs in the bedroom—Cahill making certain he heard everything that went on in there. One was hidden in the extension phone's base unit. The other had been mounted inside the wall separating the bedroom from her private bath; it was behind the light switch, dangling from a wire down inside the studs.

The last bug was in her office, again inside the telephone. Agonistes swept the storage room, the spare bedroom, the balconies, the garage, without finding any more. The whole operation took slightly more than an hour and a half.

He closed up his equipment and we went out and I closed up the house. I asked him then, "Were all the bugs fully operational?"

"Yep. Your wiseguy knew what he was doing. Not the best electronics, but a professional job of setting up. Wouldn't surprise me if he's done some bug work for cash, here and there."

We went across the street to the van. The fact that the I.T.s still worked, I was thinking, explained how Cahill had found out Nedra was missing. Runyon was the type to walk around the house talking to himself; or to sit in front of his shrine and hold a conversation with Nedra's photograph. Cahill was no mental giant, but he could put two and two together. The only problem was, he'd factored in Runyon spending so much time alone in Nedra's house and come up with the wrong equation.

I said, "Now we go to my client's place. Don't mention what we found here. As far as the Runyons are concerned, you've never even heard of Nedra Merchant."

"Why? The illegal trespass?"

"Yeah. If there *are* bugs at the Runyon house, we're all going down to the Hall of Justice to make a complaint against the wiseguy. You included, as the bug expert. I didn't tell my client and her son about the bugs here, because they might let something slip to the authorities. Then we'd be compromised and maybe the case against the wiseguy would be too."

Agonistes rolled his eyes. "First an illegal trespass, then a trip to the cop house. You got any more surprises for me?"

"No."

"Better not have. And I'd better not be hung up at the Hall all evening. I promised to take Jean to the movies."

"You won't be."

"How about you?" Agonistes asked. He was inside the van by this time, putting his equipment away in specially built and cushioned compartments. "You and your lady got plans for tonight?"

"No," I said. "No plans."

"Don't tell me you and Kerry sit home like old married folks on Saturday nights? Relationships get stale that way, you know—"

"The hell with that, George," I said too sharply.

". . . What'd I say?"

"Nothing. Forget it."

"You are still with Kerry?"

"Sure I am. Why do you ask that?"

"No reason. I just wondered."

"Did I ask you if you're still with Jean?"

"Hey, I'm sorry if I touched a raw nerve—"

"You didn't touch any goddamn nerve. Hurry up in there, will you? The sooner we get this operation finished, the sooner we can both go home."

"Right," Agonistes said. "Right."

But the look he gave me was wise and seasoned with pity.

VICTOR RUNYON WAS UP and around when we arrived at his house. Dressed in a pair of slacks and an old sweater. He didn't seem quite as zombielike today, but he was not any more communicative. He came along docilely enough when I took his arm and prodded him outside with his wife and son to meet Agonistes. He wouldn't look at anybody but me, though; and his gaze kept sliding off mine as if it were greased. When I told him about the bugs that were probably infesting his home he didn't react, didn't have anything to say. It was as if he'd lost the capacity for shock or anger. As if his obsessive love for Nedra Merchant had grown so enormous inside him it had destroyed the roots of all normal emotion.

Agonistes went inside with Matt to start the sweep. I gestured to Kay Runyon to go along, too, because I wanted to talk to her husband alone.

I said to Runyon, "If Agonistes finds listening devices inside—and he will—your wife is going to make a formal complaint against Eddie Cahill. Right away, this afternoon. Matt's a witness; he's going along too."

"Did you tell them to do that?"

"I didn't tell them to do anything. It's their decision."

"And you all think I should go too."

"Felony assault is a bigger crime than illegal trespass and eavesdropping. You press charges for that and it'll ensure Cahill is arrested, tried, convicted, and sent back to prison where he belongs."

Runyon stared out at the empty street. "You don't need me."

"I don't, no, but your family does."

"No," he said. "They'd be better off without me."

"If that's what you think, you're a bigger damn fool than I thought. They need you, man. In the worst way."

Nothing from him.

"All right," I said, "look at it this way. I think Cahill bugged Nedra's house too. Two years ago, before he went to prison the second time. His fixation for her is not only sick, it's potentially deadly. You understand what I'm saying?"

"Yes. Potentially deadly."

"You still believe she's alive and unharmed, wherever she is? That she'll come home one day?"

"I have to believe it," he said.

"Then help put Cahill away. For Nedra's sake, if not for your family's. You've got no good reason not to, Runyon."

Silence for almost a minute, while he stared again at the street. The expression on his battered face was fixed. I was not even sure he was thinking about what I'd said until he spoke again.

"All right."

"You'll come with us to the Hall of Justice? You'll file assault charges against Cahill?"

"I'll file charges," he said.

AGONISTES FOUND FOUR infinity transmitters in the Runyon house—one in each of the three phones they had, including the phone in Kay Runyon's studio, and another behind the light switch in the master bedroom. There wasn't any doubt in his mind, he said, that they'd been planted recently. They were brand-new, shiny, dust-free.

As soon as he was done, I got the Runyons into my car and drove downtown to the Hall of Justice. Agonistes followed in his van. Kay Runyon was in much better spirits; her husband's decision had relieved her and resuscitated her dying optimism. Matt was solemn. At seventeen, life is either carefree or dead-bang serious, without much shading in between. Runyon sat next to me in the front seat, not speaking, body rigid, eyes straight ahead. If he was thinking about backing out at the last minute, I wasn't going to let him do it.

At the Hall, we ran into a little luck. An inspector I knew named Branislaus was on tap in General Works, so I didn't have to go through a lot of preliminary explanations. I told Branny most of the story, with backup from Agonistes and Kay Runyon. He asked questions; we supplied answers. Runyon cooperated fully, in flat tones with plenty of candor even when the questions concerned Nedra Merchant and his relationship with her.

The whole thing took about half an hour. Then there was paperwork, and more questions to complete it—another hour. When that was done Kay Runyon asked Branislaus, "Will you arrest Cahill right away, tonight?"

"That depends on the Daly City police, and on how difficult Cahill is to pin down. I'll request a pickup-and-hold on him immediately. Then it's out of my hands."

Agonistes went home with Kay Runyon's check for five hundred dollars; she hadn't batted an eye when I told her his fee. I drove the Runyons back to Ashbury Heights. Matt and his father went straight into the house. Mrs. Runyon stayed for a few words with me.

"You'll keep looking for Nedra?" she asked.

I nodded.

"I thought you would but I wanted to be sure. If we're ever going to have Vic back, Matt and I, it won't be until he knows she's dead. Or alive and no longer available to him."

"I'll be in touch, Mrs. Runyon."

"Thank you," she said, and before she went into the house she did an odd thing: She leaned up and kissed me on the cheek. It made me feel old. And it made me feel bad, because it started me thinking again about Kerry.

I COULDN'T GO HOME, not yet, and I had no taste for restaurant food or tavern beer. Where else but to the damn office? No messages: still no word from Kerry. Unless she'd called me at home . . . but I knew I wouldn't find a message from her there either. I sat at my desk and tried to lose myself in paperwork, all there was to occupy my hands and my head at seven o'clock on a Saturday evening.

Twenty slow-moving minutes of that—and the telephone bell went off, so loud in the heavy silence that I dropped the pen I was using to sign a dun letter.

I picked up fast, knowing it wouldn't be Kerry, hoping it would be. It was Kay Runyon. Sounding upset again, frantic to the point of tears.

"It's Vic," she said.

"What about him?"

"He found where I hid his car keys. He's . . . gone."

"Take it easy. Maybe he just needed to get out for a while. Even if he went up to Crestmont—"

"You don't understand. I mean he's *gone*. He left me a note. In the bedroom, on the nightstand."

"A note? Saying what?"

"Saying good-bye."

Chapter **16**

I ASKED HER, "How long ago did he leave?"

"Within the hour. Matt had a date tonight and I went to the store. There wasn't anything to eat in the house and I thought it would be all right to leave Vic alone for a little while. . . ."

"He seemed okay when you left?"

"Yes. He was in the bedroom, lying down."

"Did he have much to say after I dropped you off?"

"More than he has lately. He said he was glad you'd talked him into signing a complaint against Cahill. He said now he didn't have to worry about anything happening to Matt and me." She made a sticky breathing sound, as if she were having respiratory difficulties. "Oh God, I'm afraid, I'm so afraid."

I didn't have to ask her why. I could hear Runyon saying to me earlier, talking about his family: *They'd be better off without me.* Deep depression, a feeling of hopelessness . . . and if he'd stopped believing finally that Nedra Merchant was alive, that she'd come back and take up with him again, you had more than a note saying good-bye. You had a man shaking hands with death.

She said, "I think he took a gun with him."

Fine, dandy. "What kind of gun?"

"I'm not sure . . . a pistol, for target shooting. He used to take Matt target shooting. It was packed away in the garage and now it's gone. I looked before I called you."

"Why didn't you tell me about the gun before?"

"He hadn't had it out in so long, I just forgot about it. Until I read that note . . ."

He didn't want to do it there, I thought, where she or Matt would find him. Nedra's house? Would he want to die there, sully the seat of his shrine? Maybe, maybe not. He was a sick man; there was no way to predict what kind of thoughts were working inside the head of a man with his type of affliction.

"I don't know what to do," Kay Runyon said. "Tell me what to do. Should I call the police?"

"Yes. As soon as we hang up. Talk to Inspector Branislaus if he's in, tell him exactly what you told me. Then call the suicide prevention hotline; their people are trained in this sort of thing."

"All right. Will you try to find him too?"

"I'll do what I can."

"That woman's house . . ."

"It's the first place I'll check."

"I was going to drive there myself," she said, "but if he's there . . . if he'd already . . . I couldn't stand to find him, to see him like that. . . ."

"You don't have to explain, Mrs. Runyon."

I heard her draw another sticky breath. "His office . . . that's another place he might have gone. Should I try to call there?"

"After you've talked to the police and suicide prevention."

"Yes, all right."

"Is there anywhere else he might be? Someplace private he goes when he wants to be by himself?"

"Mount Davidson," she said. "He . . . the monument up

there, the cross. He's always found it a peaceful place. We used to go together sometimes. . . ."

"Anyplace else?"

"I can't think of anyplace."

"Call my car phone if he comes home or you hear from him or the police. If I don't contact you, you'll know I haven't found him and I'm still looking."

I got her off the line so she could ring Branislaus. The police weren't going to do much except put out a pickup-and-hold order on Runyon, but it would have been cruel to tell her that. Cops are overworked, especially on summer Saturday nights, and all she had to give them was a husband gone for one hour, a missing target pistol, and an uncorroborated suspicion that he intended to do himself harm; he'd never even mentioned suicide to her or she'd have told me about it. The suicide prevention people couldn't do much either, except to help hold her together. If anybody tracked down Victor Runyon before he pulled the trigger on himself—or afterward—the chances were it would be me.

HE WASN'T AT NEDRA MERCHANT'S HOUSE. No sign of his BMW on Crestmont, and the place was dark and still locked up tight. But I parked and went in to check it anyway, just to make sure.

While I was at the door, a car rolled uphill and then swung over directly in front of the gate, on the side of the street where you weren't supposed to park. I recrossed the deck, went through the gate. The car was a new, beige Cadillac Eldorado, and the man getting out of it was Walter Merchant.

We both stopped and looked at each other, him with one hand holding the car door open. His expression said he was puzzled, concerned, and a little sheepish. The bright glaze on his eyes said he'd been out liquor tasting. He wasn't hammered, but he wasn't sober either.

"What're you doing here, Mr. Merchant?"

"I might ask you the same thing." No word-slur, at least.

"Looking for somebody on behalf of my client."

"One of her conquests?"

"Who I'm looking for is my business."

"Wouldn't have anything to do with Nedra's disappearance, would it?"

"No, it wouldn't. I told you I'd let you know if I found out what happened to her. I haven't; I still don't have a clue. Now, why are you here?"

He let out a boozy sigh. "I can't give you much of an answer, I'm afraid. I've been for drinks with a client who lives over on Parnassus. That's not far away and on my way home I thought, well, why not?" He chuckled self-deprecatingly. "Oh, hell, I don't know. Nedra's been on my mind ever since you told me she was missing."

"You come up here often, do you?"

"Christ, no. This is the first time in years."

"Uh-huh."

"The truth, whether you believe it or not. I was married to the woman for five years, lived with her in this house for five years. I'm concerned about her—you can understand that, can't you?"

I could understand it, all right. His torch was burning hot again after years of being dampered down to a sizzle; hell, I was the one who'd relit it for him. So now here he was, mooning around up here too. Runyon and Cahill and now Merchant—a regular goddamn convention of bewitched males making pilgrimages to the lair of the enchantress.

Merchant said, "You leaving now?"

"That's right."

"Me too. Home and hearth await."

"Maybe you'd better sit here for a while. Or go for a walk, get some fresh air."

"I'm sober enough to drive."

"Are you? The legal limit is point-oh-eight and you're carrying more than that for sure."

"Never cite the law to a lawyer," he said.

He got into the car. I thought about reaching in, yanking his keys out of the ignition; but it would probably mean laying hands on him, and he was litigious as hell. I might have done it anyway, but I'd waited too long: he slammed the door and I heard the lock click.

I leaned down to the window. "Don't kill anybody on your way home."

He pulled a face—half smile and half grimace—saluted, and put the car in gear. The U-turn he executed was slow and careful; so was his progress around the first curve and out of sight. So maybe he wouldn't kill anybody on the way home, himself included—the damn fool.

MOUNT DAVIDSON WAS only a few miles from Mount Sutro; I went up there next. Highest hill in San Francisco at over nine hundred feet, and atop it, one of the city's manmade parks dominated by the huge cross where Easter morning services are held every year. Lonely enough spot at night, despite regular police patrols—just the sort of place that might attract a potential suicide. But not Victor Runyon, at least not this soon after nightfall. None of the cars parked up there was a BMW.

Downtown. SoMa was jumping: bright lights, restless crowds, and just about any kind of night action you wanted, from stand-up comedians to sadomasochistic gay sex shows performed by leather-clad men in cages. The building in which Runyon had his business office was shut down, but there was a security guard in residence. He knew Runyon, he said. And hadn't seen him in over a week. He assured me that there was no way Runyon could have gotten into the building tonight unseen.

Getting on toward ten o'clock now. I headed up Market: no place to go except back to Crestmont, start all over again. Nights like this, on missions like this, I felt like a hunk of metal hurtling through black space. Moving at speed, veering off on tangents now and then, sometimes traveling in circles, but without any real destination or purpose in the scheme of the universe; lighted objects all around, some close, some remote, none with any connection to me—other fragments rushing on their aimless courses, different and yet fundamentally the same. A small, useless thing, all alone on a zigzag course toward the edge of the void.

Bad thinking—bad anytime. I switched on the radio to get some distracting noise into the car. Drive, just drive, don't think.

Crestmont, the red-shingled house. Still no sign of Runyon.

Mount Davidson. Still no sign of Runyon.

I came down out of the park on Dalewood, swung over and got onto Portola Drive. But instead of heading down Market again, I turned on Diamond Heights Boulevard. Useless to go to SoMa again; he wasn't going to be at his office now either. Out driving around somewhere, maybe, trying to work up enough nerve to blow himself away. Or already dead in some other private place. Why the hell keep chasing around the way I had been? Why try to stop him at all? Just let the poor bastard do it, if he hadn't already. He was no good to his family anymore, likely never would be again; and worst of all, he was no good to himself. Everybody concerned would be better off with him dead and gone.

But I didn't believe it. I was not that cynical—not yet. Busted-up humans like Runyon could be fixed; and even if they couldn't, the people who loved them had the moral right to keep them alive. In Runyon's case, I had the moral obligation to help his loved ones keep him alive. I had played the vengeful god once, not long ago: decided spur-of-the-moment that the world would be better off with a man dead and then made him that way. The man had been evil, but that didn't make what I'd done right; just, maybe, but not right. It was a decision and a responsibility I never wanted to be mine again.

Back to SoMa, then, and the whole circuit a third time if necessary. But not just yet. First, a little detour up Gold Mine Drive.

KERRY WASN'T HOME.

I didn't see her car on two passes, and when I U-turned and came back again I parked in front of her building and went into the foyer and rang her bell. I could have let myself in with my key; I could have gone into her apartment and poked around to see if there was any evidence of an affair with Paul Blessing. I even thought for a few seconds about doing just that. But I couldn't go through with it, any more than I could drive over to Tiburon and see if she was with Blessing at his house. Or come back here later and hang around to find out if she came home.

I did not want to learn the truth in any of those ways, on the sly, like the sleazy keyhole peepers and divorce mucksters that had given my profession a bad name. I had too much respect for Kerry, for what we'd had together, for myself, to invade her privacy and turn a painful situation into an ugly one. A little dignity isn't much to hang on to when a relationship starts to come apart, but it's something at least. Something important.

A LITTLE DIGNITY.

The phrase kept repeating itself in my mind as I drove—and I had a sudden insight into Eberhardt, into what had made him quit me the way he had.

It wasn't freedom he'd wanted; it was dignity.

It wasn't that he'd grown to dislike me; it was that I stood in the way of him liking himself.

He'd put thirty years of his life into being a cop, a good honest cop, and frustrations and dissatisfactions had built up, and one day six years ago he'd made a sudden moral decision—just as I had in causing an evil man's death—that went against everything he was and believed in. He'd let himself take a bribe. He changed his mind at the last minute, tried to back out of the deal, and that had spurred the briber to hire someone to murder him. The fact that he'd been shot down and nearly killed should have been punishment enough for his actions, but it wasn't. He couldn't reconcile the fact that he'd disgraced himself and his badge. Or that he'd compounded his guilt by not confessing to his superiors, by requesting an early retirement instead so he could keep his pension.

I was part of the problem, too, a large part. I chanced to be at his house when the hired gun showed up, and I'd also been shot and wounded. One more burden for him to bear: his fall from grace had nearly cost me my life as well as his own. Then there was the capper: I'd recovered first and gone hunting the people responsible, and in the process learned the truth about the bribe. Before long I was the only one besides Eberhardt who did know.

And yet, after he left the force he'd accepted my offer of a partnership because he had no other options. He'd thought he could live with the arrangement, but five-plus years of sharing an office and spending off-hours together had worn him down. I was a constant nagging reminder of the act he couldn't forget, couldn't forgive himself for. He must have seen himself as a loser, a sellout; and as he approached sixty, the feelings had grown more painful, less tolerable. He looked into the future and all he saw was more of the same. The grand-scale wedding to Bobbie Jean he'd planned in April had been a last-ditch effort to add some substance to his life; but he'd carried it too far and the whole thing had collapsed around him. Another loss, another failure. And I'd made it even worse by berating him, then losing my head and sucker-punching him in his own kitchen to end a heated argument.

He *had* to get shut of me after that; it had just been a matter of time. It was the only way he could go on living with himself. And once he was free of me, opening his own agency—taking charge of what remained of his life—was the only way he could recapture some of his self-worth.

The more I thought about it, the more I felt sure I'd hit on the truth. The insight made me feel something other than anger for the first time since he'd walked out; it made me sad and it made me hurt for him. It also made me want to go see him, tell him I understood now, tell him I wished him well. But it was too late for any gesture like that. He wouldn't have wanted to hear it from me. He had too much pride.

Eb, I thought, goddamn it, Eb, it wasn't just you. It wasn't just me. Life does it to all of us, one way or another. Nobody can exist in a perfect vacuum, without some sin, some shame. There are no saints anymore, if there ever were.

But he wouldn't have wanted to hear that either.

I DROVE THE CITY until nearly two A.M., back and forth from Forest Hill to Mount Davidson to SoMa. No Victor Runyon. And no call from his wife.

Fatigue and hunger prodded me home finally. I didn't feel like eating, but the pains in my belly were hot and insistent—I hadn't had any food in eighteen hours—and I was afraid of doing some harm to myself. I forced down a sandwich. Half an apple, too, before I fell asleep sitting at the kitchen table.

Chapter **17**

THE TELEPHONE RANG just as I was getting out of the shower. I
hoped it would be Kerry, thought it was probably Kay Runyon; it
was neither. Inspector Branislaus, SFPD.

"Wake you up?" he asked.

"No. I've been up for a while."

"Six o'clock for me. On a Sunday morning that's obscene.
I hate pulling weekend duty."

"What's up, Branny? You find Runyon?"

"Not yet, alive or dead. No, I'm calling about Eddie Cahill.
I thought you'd want to know."

"Know what? Don't tell me he's still on the loose?"

"Afraid so. Daly City officers went out to his address last
night and he wasn't there. They waited around quite a while, but
he didn't show. Early this morning they went back. He was there,
but when they tried to take him into custody he assaulted one of
the officers and got away."

"In the van or on foot?"

"On foot. They brought cars into the area pretty fast, but he
still managed to slip through."

"Armed?"

"We don't know. Officers got a warrant and searched the house and there weren't any weapons or spare rounds. But that doesn't have to mean anything. What they did find was electronics equipment—the surveillance kind, including some of the same bugs Agonistes found in the Runyon house. The old phone company ID too."

"Hard evidence."

"Right. He'll go up for sure once we nail him."

"He might try to contact his sister," I said. "Ask her to hide him out or help him leave the city."

"I already talked to the brother-in-law," Branislaus said. "He doesn't like Cahill; he'll turn him in if he has the chance."

"Runyon's wife know about this yet?"

"Yeah. She called here ten minutes ago. I figured she had a right to know."

"How'd she take it?"

"She seemed numb. All she can think about is her husband."

"Can you spare somebody to keep an eye on her and her son until Cahill's picked up?"

"I wish I could. But we're shorthanded. Hell, when aren't we?"

"I'll do it, then. Keep me posted, Branny."

"Will do."

I had drip-dried, talking to him. I threw the bath towel into the hamper and got dressed and went into the kitchen for another cup of coffee. Breakfast? I felt that I ought to eat something, but there was nothing in the fridge that appealed to me. I didn't want to hang around here anyway. Too much time alone with myself the past eighteen hours; this was a day I needed to spend among people, even if they were all relative strangers.

ZIM'S ON VAN NESS was where I went to eat. The food made no impression on me; I forgot what it was even as I was shoveling it down. The place was crowded, though, and when I came out afterward there was a congestion of cars in the area: morning mass at St. Mary's, on Cathedral Hill nearby, had just let out. The good clear sound of church bells filled the warm Sunday morning. The people and the bells made me feel better than I had in a while.

I walked down O'Farrell to my office. One thing to take care of there before I drove to Ashbury Heights to see how Kay Runyon was holding up. As I walked, I had a mental image of the nave of St. Mary's—the old church that had been destroyed by fire in 1962. Only once had I been inside the huge new cathedral that had opened in 1971, and that had been to see what it was like, not to attend services. More than thirty years since I'd been to mass at St. Mary's or any other church, even though Cathedral Hill was only a few blocks from my flat. Long, long time. My ma had been a devout Catholic, had tried to raise me the same way; I'd gone along with her wishes to please her, but after she died, religion had no longer meant much to me. Such a good woman, so devout, and all she'd got for her virtue and her faith had been pain and suffering. God's fault or not? For a long time I'd thought it was; now I wasn't so sure. Might do me some good to give Him another chance . . . go to services again . . . take some of the old teachings to heart.

Might, yes, if I could learn to believe again. But could I, after so many years? Religion is no comfort at all without faith, and I was no longer even sure I had faith in myself, let alone in a higher power.

Something to think about. One more thing to think about. . . .

My building was deserted, as usual on Sundays. When I let myself into the office I stood for a few seconds, listening. The only sounds were from outside the building; inside, there was dead silence. No creaks, no groans, no ghostly complaints. Only at night, and no mistake. Just another of life's little mysteries.

The message light on my answering machine wasn't blinking. So Annette Olroyd had yet to respond to the request I'd left with her mother. Still out of town? Or it could be she'd got back too late last night to call and hadn't had a chance yet this morning. I looked up her number, tapped it out.

Six rings, and a female voice said, "Hello?" Not the mother's; this one was younger, and tiny like a munchkin's, and diffident.

"Ms. Olroyd? Annette Olroyd?"

Brief pause before she said guardedly, "Yes?"

I identified myself. "I spoke to your mother yesterday, about the postcards you received from Nedra Merchant. Did she tell you about our conversation?"

Ongoing silence. I couldn't even hear her breathing. The line was still open, though; faint circuit noises tickled my ear.

"Ms. Olroyd?"

"My mother," she said, "is too trusting."

". . . I'm sorry?"

"With strangers. In person and on the phone."

"If you think she betrayed a confidence—"

"Didn't she?"

"No. She was candid and helpful, that's all."

"I don't know you," the woman said.

"I'm a licensed private investigator—"

"I know *that*. I looked up the name in the phone book. But I don't know *you*. How can I be certain you're who you say you are?"

Paranoid, I thought. With or without good reason, like a lot of people these days. "I can prove it to you easily enough," I said, trying to sound reassuring, "if you'll just—"

"I'm not going to give you my address," she said. "At least my mother didn't go that far."

"Would you like to come to my office?"

Pause. "No, I don't think so."

"And you won't tell me about the postcards on the phone."

"No. Why do you want to find Nedra? You didn't tell my mother your reasons."

"I think she might be in serious trouble. You know that she dropped out of sight suddenly—"

"She explained that on her first card."

"In detail?"

". . . No. Not in detail. But she wrote the cards, they're in her handwriting. She's perfectly fine."

"Is she, Ms. Olroyd? A person's handwriting can be duplicated, you know."

Silence.

"Or she might have written the cards under duress. Has that possibility occurred to you?"

More silence. Thinking it over, I hoped.

"If you care at all about Nedra Merchant," I said, "please help me. We could meet in a public place, if you'd rather not come to my office. Anyplace you like—you name it."

". . . I can't this morning," she said. Weakening; it was in her voice. "I have things to do, I don't know how long they'll take. I was just about to leave when you called."

"This afternoon, then. Whatever time is convenient for you."

"Well, after two o'clock . . ."

"Two-thirty? Three?"

"Three," she said.

"Where would you feel comfortable meeting?"

"There's a . . ." she began, and then stopped and then made a throat-clearing sound. "Do you know Mountain Lake Park?"

"Off Lake Street, edge of the Presidio?"

"Yes. We could meet there."

"Fine. Where in the park?"

"The Eleventh Avenue entrance . . . there's a big rock in the grass, halfway between the entrance and the lake. It has a plaque on it, to a Spanish explorer."

"Rock with a plaque, right. You want to tell me what you look like? Or would you rather I described myself?"

"You tell me," she said.

"Late sixties, dark, heavyset, graying hair. Wearing a brown sport jacket, beige slacks, a blue shirt without a tie. All right?"

"Yes . . . all right."

"You do still have the postcards?"

"I still have them."

"If you'd bring them along, let me take a look at them, it would be a big help. Will you do that?"

". . . I suppose so."

"Three o'clock, Ms. Olroyd. Please don't disappoint me. For Nedra's sake."

"Three o'clock," she said in her tiny munchkin's voice, and hung up without saying good-bye.

I was sweating a little as I cradled the receiver. Talking to people like Annette Olroyd is hard work.

The phone bell jangled as I was getting out of my chair. Kerry, I thought. Immediate reaction these days, like one of Pavlov's drooling dogs. And the same letdown when I heard somebody else's voice. Kay Runyon was the only woman interested in talking to me lately, it seemed.

"I called your home number," she said, "and I called your car phone." She sounded apprehensive but not quite as frantic as she had yesterday evening. "I didn't think you'd be in your office on Sunday."

"It's just another day to me. Everything okay?"

"Yes. But I'd like to see you. Can you come here?"

"I'd already planned on it. You haven't had any word on your husband?"

"No, it's not that. It's just . . . I need to see you. Will you come right away?"

"As soon as I can."

"Please hurry," she said, and rang off.

More hard work coming up.

THERE WAS PLENTY of Sunday activity in Ashbury Heights, including a family of badminton players swatting a shuttlecock back and forth over a net strung across their tiny front lawn. Drapes and windows were open all along the winding street, to let in the sun and the warm, breezeless air—but not at the Runyon house. Huddled away in there already, I thought: mourners before the fact.

I parked in front, went up and rang the bell. The door opened in two seconds flat, as if Matt had been lurking behind it with his hand on the knob. He was strung tight this morning, so tight he was almost quivering. There was something in his face, too, that I couldn't read because he put his back to me almost immediately, without speaking, and walked away into the Dreamsicle living room.

He stopped half a dozen paces into the room; I stopped in the doorway, with a sudden shriveling sensation in my belly and groin. Now I knew what had been in the boy's face, why he was drawn so tight.

Kay Runyon wasn't alone in there. Eddie Cahill stood behind the orange-and-white couch she was sitting on, the muzzle of a Saturday night special pressed against her right temple.

Chapter  18

CAHILL SAID, "Come on in here, slick. Nice and slow."

I moved ahead, halfway to the couch before I stopped again. You could feel the strain in there, the hard scraping edge of tension, but it wasn't as acute as it might have been. Cahill was keyed up, sweating, but he seemed to have the furnace of violence in him under control. Kay Runyon was calm; there was no panic in her eyes, only a dull fright. She had been through so much recently, her sensibilities bludgeoned and bruised to the point of numbness. I felt bad for her, and bad for Matt, and angry as hell at the half-wit with the gun.

I asked her, "You okay, Mrs. Runyon?"

"Yes." Low voice, as stunned as her eyes.

"He didn't hurt you?"

"No."

"How long has he been here?"

"More than an hour . . . just before he made me call you. He forced his way in—"

"Shut up," Cahill said. His gaze, when he shifted it to me,

showed more heat. "Don't talk to her, goddamn it. You talk to me."

"I don't have anything to say to you."

"That's what you think. You carrying heat?"

"No."

"Show me."

I opened my jacket, fanned it up and out, and did a slow turn. "Satisfied?"

"Go stand next to the kid."

I went over beside Matt. His hands were fisted at his sides, locked down rigid; when I glanced at him I could see his neck cords bulging, the pulse throbbing in the hollow of his throat, the faint forward straining of his body. Like a pit bull at the end of a leash, I thought. Release him and he'd try to tear Cahill apart.

I said to Cahill, "What's this all about?"

"You know what it's about. You fuckers sicced the cops on me, you and Runyon. Richie told me that."

"Richie?"

"My fuggin brother-in-law. He turned my own sister against me. A few bucks and a set of wheels, that's all I wanted; but no, Richie drags out his piece"—he waggled the Saturday night special—"and sticks it in my face. Would of shot me, too, if I hadn't taken it away from him. Fixed *his* wagon for him, the bastard."

"What'd you do to him?"

"Busted his head," Cahill said. "Gave Marj a jolt too. That's what she gets for marrying Richie. A spic—what's she want to marry a fuggin spic for anyway?"

His smooth red face turned brooding and petulant; you could see his emotions running naked there. He'd backed himself into a corner, not for the first time in his miserable life, but he didn't see it that way. It was always somebody else's fault—in this case, the Runyons', mine, his sister's, his brother-in-law's. Angry, persecuted, trapped, and not very bright, with no place to run and no place to hide, taking out his frustrations on the people he blamed for his trouble.

But that still didn't explain why he'd come here. This was a
bigger risk than anything else he might have done—

Runyon, I thought, that's why. He's after Runyon.

And Nedra. Even now, on the run, he can't let go of his
fixation for her.

"Here's the way it stacks up," he said. "You give me what
I want and I walk out of here and nobody gets hurt."

"I can't give you what you want. None of us can."

"No? I'm talking about Runyon."

"I know what you're talking about."

"I told him we don't know where Vic is," Kay Runyon
said. "I told him and Matt told him, but he won't believe us."

"It's the truth, Cahill. They don't know and I don't know
either."

"You got to have some idea."

"No. If I had, don't you think I'd have been out working on
it instead of sitting around my office this morning?"

He shook his head stubbornly; he had one thought in there
and by God nothing and nobody was going to drive it out. "You
people put me on the run—okay, that's over and done with. But I
ain't going anywhere until I find out what he did to Nedra."

I asked Kay Runyon, "Did you show him the note your
husband left you?"

"Yes."

"That note don't mean shit," Cahill said.

"It means he's not coming back. It means he may already
have done away with himself. What good is it going to do you to
hang around here waiting?"

"I ain't gonna hang around here long. Neither are you. You
don't know where Runyon is, all right, then you go find him and
bring him here."

"Jesus Christ, how am I going to do that? I just told you, he
may already be dead—"

"He's not dead. I don't buy that."

"I've been hunting him ever since he left last night. So have the police. Nobody has any idea where he is. How the hell can I find him if I don't know where to look?''

"I don't care how you do it, just do it."

It was like trying to talk to a wall. I felt bitterly helpless. I couldn't walk out of here and leave the woman and her son at Cahill's mercy, not unless I was prepared to go straight to the police and put their lives in further jeopardy by turning this into a SWAT-team fiasco; and I couldn't stay here because there was no way to negotiate with a monomaniacal simpleton, and no way I could see to disarm him by myself.

One more try: "It's Nedra you really want, Cahill, we both know that."

"I want to know what he did to her. She better be alive."

"I think she is. I've got an appointment with somebody later this afternoon, a friend of Nedra's who might know where to find her."

"Who? What friend?"

"I won't tell you that. But I'll take you with me when I see her—just the two of us. That's my condition: Leave Mrs. Runyon and her son here and I'll take you to the friend."

"Bullshit," Cahill said.

"What's bullshit?"

"There's no friend."

"There's a friend. I swear it."

"Then go get her and bring her here."

"I can't do that. You know I can't do that."

"Find out what the friend knows, come back and tell me."

"And then what?"

"I go find Nedra myself."

And if she's dead and you still believe Runyon did it, I thought, and Runyon still hasn't been found, you come back here and throw down on these poor people again. No way. You don't get Annette Olroyd and you don't get whatever those postcards of hers reveal.

Cahill said impatiently, "How about it, slick?"

It's got to be the cops, I thought. Walk out, call Branislaus, tell him the way it's shaped up in here. He'll take over, do what has to be done.

And if this airhead shoots Kay or Matt before the negotiators can talk him out? I couldn't live with that on my conscience.

But there's no other way. . . .

One other way: Leave, drive off, park somewhere out of sight, take the gun from the car and come back and try to get in quietly through the backyard and kitchen door, try to surprise him and pop him before he has a chance to use his weapon.

Sure, sure, big clumsy guy like me, make noise when I breathe—I couldn't sneak up on a brass band. Bigger chance of the Runyons getting hurt that way than with trained hostage negotiators handling it. I'm no hero, for Christ's sake, especially not with other people's lives at stake.

"Come on, slick," Cahill said, "make up your fuggin mind." Angry now, letting the doors to the furnace blow open. He moved a pace to his right, took the Saturday night special away from Kay Runyon's head so he could jam it in my direction for emphasis. His eyes had fire in them now—the meltdown glare, bright and crackling and all for me.

And that was good because he didn't see Matt move. He didn't but I did—a slow, sideways shifting that brought the boy up next to a spindly table with an orange pottery vase on it. There were maybe fifteen feet separating him and Cahill.

I knew instantly what was in the kid's mind and I wanted to yell at him not to do it; reach over and grab him and haul him down before he acted. But any sudden cry or activity on my part would probably trigger Cahill. Nothing for me to do but keep Cahill's attention centered on me and then attack when Matt attacked.

"Listen to me, Cahill," I said. "You're making a big mistake."

"You listen, slick. You shag ass out of here right now, no more crap, or I hurt these two. You understand me?"

Matt's hand was on the vase.

"Suppose I don't?" I said. "You going to shoot me down in cold blood?"

"Maybe. You want to find out?"

"You ever killed anybody, Cahill? No, I don't think so. Not with a gun anyway. You're not that cold-blooded."

"You don't know me, you don't know what—"

Matt swung the vase up and chucked it, all in one quick blurred motion. Oh yeah, a ballplayer—a good one, thank God. The vase slammed into the side of Cahill's head, knocked him sideways and his hot eyes out of focus. The crack of the pottery shattering and Cahill's pained bellow and Kay Runyon's startled cry all seemed magnified, like eruptions blowing away the silence.

Matt was closer to Cahill and I had the couch to get around; he got there first, hurling himself at the bigger man just as the gun came up in Cahill's hand. The thing went off and Kay Runyon screamed, but the muzzle was pointed downward; the bullet burrowed harmlessly into the floor.

The force of the kid's lunge drove both of them, reeling, into the far wall. They bounced off, into another table; the table buckled and collapsed under their combined weight, brought them down with it in a tangle of arms and legs and broken wood. I saw the Saturday night special pop loose from Cahill's grasp, but when I went after it somebody's leg flailed out and tripped me, sent me sprawling into the back of the couch. Kay Runyon made another noise; I heard Cahill say "Shit!" explosively. I got my footing back, turned in time to see him punch Matt over the eye and break free. He looked for the gun, but I was already lunging for it. I scooped it up, swung around with my finger sliding through the trigger guard.

Cahill wasn't going to fight me for it. Coward underneath all that hard-ass exterior: he'd turned tail and was running for the hallway.

I yelled for him to stop but he didn't break stride; he veered away from the front door, though, instinctively realizing I could see him if he tried to get out that way, take a clear shot at his back. He charged ahead into the kitchen. I started after him, but Matt was on his feet by then and between me and the hall. His mother and I both shouted his name, a half-beat apart so that the effect was of an echo. He didn't listen to either of us. Just pelted, head down, in Cahill's wake.

I lumbered around the couch, got past Kay Runyon. "Stay here, call nine-eleven," I told her, and ran on through the hall into the kitchen.

It was empty; Matt had just slammed out the back door. I yanked the thing open, went onto the porch. Cahill was off to the right of the studio, barreling across the lawn toward the fence that separated the Runyon property from the pedestrian ladder street beyond. Matt was twenty yards behind him and gaining.

At first I thought Cahill would slacken speed and jump for the top of the fence, try to scale it. But no, he kept right on going full tilt toward the access door. He hit it like a bull smacking into a bullring wall: head lowered, shoulder up, legs driving. The lock burst loose in a shriek of metal and wood, the door flew outward, boards splintered loose from the fence and the whole thing wobbled and sagged. Somehow Cahill kept his balance, turned uphill on the ladder street. Matt was right behind him. I could hear the two of them pounding up the steps as I ran across the yard.

When I came out onto the street and looked upward, Cahill was on the concrete halfway up, trying to use the iron side railing to give himself greater impetus. But Matt was younger, faster; he caught Cahill by the shirt, yanked him back and around, and smacked him full in the face. I saw blood spurt, heard Cahill roar with pain. Then they were locked together, slugging at each other; and then they were down on the landing, rolling around in an even more frantic embrace.

Cahill had the greater strength, would have won the wrestling match inside of two minutes. But I was up there with them in less than one, jockeying to stay out of harm's way so I could draw a bead on Cahill's head. He gave me the opening I was after when he rolled on top of the boy and reared back to throw a punch. I clouted him on the right ear with the flat barrel of the

Saturday night special. It stunned him; a grunt came out of his
throat and he tried jerkily to turn my way. I clubbed him again,
and a third time as he was toppling sideways. The third blow laid
him out facedown on the dirty concrete, kept him there.

There was a shout from near the top of the hill. A bearded
guy had his head poked over a privet hedge, peering down at us.
"What the hell's going on down there?"

I called back, "Dangerous police situation, don't interfere,"
and his head vanished instantly. I could hear other voices now,
here and there in the vicinity, and they kept up an intermittent
chatter. But nobody else ventured out onto the ladder street,
wholly or in part.

I looked over at Matt. He was sucking at a knuckle, his eyes
still bright with rage.

"You okay?" I asked him.

"Yeah, sure," he said. His shirt was torn, one arm and one
cheek were gouged and bleeding, and he was going to have a
honey of a black eye before long. "You?"

"Pretty good now."

"I hope you busted his fucking skull."

"I didn't hit him that hard. You took a stupid damn chance,
jumping him like that inside. And then chasing him out here. You
could have got yourself killed."

"Yeah, well, I couldn't take it anymore. I had enough of his
crap. You know?"

"I know," I said. "Real well."

"You want me to call the cops?"

"Your mother should already have done that. You better go
and tell her you're all right." I shifted the Saturday night special
to my left hand, hauled my keys out and gave them to Matt.
"Then go out to my car and bring the handcuffs from the trunk.
They're in a box in there."

"Right." He trotted away down the steps.

I sat in a patch of warm sunlight and listened to the neighbors and watched Cahill. He was beginning to stir around. Pretty
soon he lifted himself onto all fours, raised his head. His nose

was bent and crooked, leaking blood; Matt had busted it as effectively as Cahill had busted his father's. When his eyes cleared and he saw me he tensed, started to pull his feet under him.

"Don't even think about it, slick," I said. "I'll shoot your eye out if you don't sit still and keep your mouth shut. Believe it. It'd be a pleasure."

He believed it. He sat still and kept his mouth shut, before and after Matt brought the handcuffs.

Chapter **19**

NARROW AND SEVERAL BLOCKS LONG, Mountain Lake Park is tucked away behind Lake Street apartment buildings and stands of tall cypress and eucalyptus. The little lake there reaches up into a corner of the Presidio army base. It used to be called Laguna de Loma Alta, Lake of the High Hill, after the Presidio's four-hundred-foot elevation; "Mountain Lake" is a poor substitute. Thick shrubbery rims it to the waterline, except for a thin stretch of beach on the south end. Ducks, swans, and patches of tule grass occupy its relatively clean waters. Soothing, well used, and safe in daylight—that's Mountain Lake Park. Just the kind of place where a paranoid munchkin would feel secure.

I got there just past four. My meeting with Annette Olroyd was supposed to have been at three, but the law had kept me at the Runyon house until three-thirty. Branislaus had come out, among others, and before and after Eddie Cahill had been carted off to jail there were strings of questions to answer. When I saw I wasn't going to get away in time to keep the three o'clock appointment, I'd called Ms. Olroyd and switched the time. She hadn't liked that, but I'd soft-talked her into it. It was even money as to whether or not she would actually show up.

I parked on the short section of Eleventh Avenue that dead-ends at the park, walked across gopher-hole-pocked grass toward the lake. There were a lot of people around, walking and running and bicycling; tennis players exerted themselves on the nearby courts and kids made a racket in the playground farther down. Not as many as there would have been earlier though. Fog was starting to sift in from the ocean and a wind had sprung up and the day was turning chill. In another hour the sky would be a sullen gray, the wind salt-sharp and numbing.

I found the big rock with no trouble; it was the only one around. The plaque embedded in it said that Juan Bautista De-Anza had camped on this spot a couple of hundred years ago and that in 1957 the Daughters of American Colonists had considered the fact to be worthy of commemoration. I doubted that one in fifty thousand users of the park had ever heard of Juan Bautista de Anza, much less knew what it was he'd accomplished. It made me a little sheepish to realize I wasn't the one exception. I sat down on his memorial, thinking wryly that at least somebody had remembered him; nobody was going to remember me a couple of hundred hours, let alone a couple of hundred years, after I croaked. Or erect anything in my memory except a headstone.

Not far away, a lean, homely dog was snagging a Frisbee tossed by a guy wearing a Grateful Dead T-shirt—both of them in defiance of the park's leash law. That dog could really get up off the ground, a sort of canine version of Michael Jordan elevating for a slam-dunk. Air Dog. I watched him until his owner got tired of the game and the mutt wandered off to take a dump in some bushes. Then the Grateful Dead guy and I both pretended Air Dog had temporarily ceased to exist.

I looked out over the lake and listened to the steady hum of traffic on Park Presidio Boulevard and thought about Eddie Cahill. Close call in Ashbury Heights earlier; it was a small miracle nobody had been hurt except Cahill. I couldn't find too much fault with Matt Runyon, though. He was a good kid, if too impulsive for his own good. His mother's son, not his father's: strong, tough inside where it counted. He'd get through this ugly time without too many scars. So would Kay Runyon. Or maybe I just wanted to think that was how it would be for both of them.

Victor Runyon. Dead yet or not?

Nedra Adams Merchant. Dead or not?

My relationship with Kerry. Dead or not?

I shifted around on the rock and looked at my watch. Ten after four. The fog was rolling in fast now; a gust of wind bothered my hair and made me shiver. Air Dog and Grateful Dead were heading out toward Lake Street. So were several others.

Come on, lady, I thought—and behind me, not too far away, a tentative voice said my name.

I craned my head around. A woman in a knee-length blue coat was standing there peering at me through a pair of gold-rimmed glasses. I hadn't heard her approach; she'd come over grass and she walked soft. I wondered how long she'd been standing there studying me, making up her mind.

I said, "Yes, that's me. Ms. Olroyd?"

She nodded and came forward hesitantly and stopped again about three feet away. She had no intention of sharing the rock with me. She was about forty, thin, ash-blond—not unattractive except for the fact that she wore about a pound of makeup. Bright red lipstick, green and purple eyeshadow, rouge on her cheeks . . . as if, consciously or unconsciously, she'd constructed a mask to hide behind.

She said in her munchkin's voice, "May I see some identification, please?" Not quite making eye contact as she spoke.

"Of course."

I produced my wallet and opened it to the Photostat of my license and leaned forward to hand it to her. She took it carefully, so as to avoid touching my hand; squinted at the license for a full thirty seconds before she returned the wallet.

"Okay?" I said.

"Yes."

I put the wallet away, smiling at her. She didn't smile back. "Thank you for coming, Ms. Olroyd. I appreciate it."

"For Nedra's sake," she said. "That's the only reason I'm here."

"Me too."

A little silence. Then: "Do you honestly believe the postcards will help you find her?"

"They might, yes. Did you bring them?"

"Yes."

"May I see them?"

She opened a canvas handbag, peered inside, brought out a pair of cards. Held them for a few seconds, as if she couldn't bear to let go of them, and then thrust them in my direction—again without making eye contact.

Two standard-size picture postcards, one labeled *Clear Lake* and depicting an aerial view of that large body of water and its surrounding hills, the other labeled *Lakeport* and showing a cluttered view of the town's municipal pier and boat harbor. I turned them over. The postmark on one was smeared and unreadable; the postmark on the other read "Lucerne CA 95458."

"Well?" Annette Olroyd said.

I didn't answer her. I was reading the messages written on the cards, one in purple ink, the other in blue ink. The handwriting was the same on both, but firmer and deeply indented into the card on the older of the two, dated June 10, as if it had been written in anger or some other strong emotional state. The words on that one said:

Dear Annette—

Greetings from Clear Lake. I'm sorry I didn't call you before I left the city, but I needed to get away for a while. Personal reasons. Don't worry about me, I'm fine. I don't know when I'll be back, probably not for a while. I'll call you then.

Nedra

The other card, dated July 9, was a little shaky, as if Nedra hadn't been feeling well that day. Its message was briefer and even more nonspecific:

Dear Annette—
  Just a note to let you know I'm fine and thinking of you. See you soon.

                                                            Nedra

I looked up and caught Annette Olroyd's eye; she lowered her gaze immediately. "Well?" she said again.

"Did Nedra ever mention Clear Lake or Lakeport to you? In person, I mean."

"No, I'm sure she didn't."

"So you don't know where she might have been staying when she wrote these cards?"

"No."

"Not even a guess?"

"I said no." Her voice rose querulously on the last word. She put her hand out. "May I please have the cards back?"

I laid the postcards on her palm. My fingers brushed her skin; she jerked away from me as if I'd burned or contaminated her. Timorous, paranoid, afraid of the male animal . . . Nedra Merchant hadn't helped her much after all. I wondered if she'd always been like that, or if the husband who'd left her had been responsible. If it was the husband, he must be a piece of work— one of the breed of men who would have served society best if they'd been castrated at birth.

She said, "I'll be going now," and stuffed the cards into her handbag. "When you find Nedra . . ." She let the sentence trail off, staring over the wind-ruffled water.

"Yes, Ms. Olroyd?"

"Please ask her to call me. I need . . . I'd like to talk to her. Will you do that?"

"Of course." If she's alive, I thought.

"Thank you."

And away she went, body drawn in and shoulders hunched against the wind. I waited until she reached the Eleventh Avenue entrance before I headed out myself. I didn't want to add to her anxiety by following too close.

AT THE OFFICE I keep an accumulation of California city and county maps. I drove there from the park and rummaged up the map for Lake County and spread it open on my desk.

Lake is a small, mountainous county a hundred miles or so northeast of San Francisco. A resort county: vacation tourism is its main industry, far outdistancing pears, walnuts, grapes, and other agricultural crops. Clear Lake dominates it—geographically, demographically, and economically. With more than a hundred miles of shoreline, it's the largest natural lake in the state, Tahoe being bigger but partially in Nevada. Lakeport, on the west shore, is the county seat and largest town with some fifteen thousand year-round residents. The population of the entire county is only slightly more than fifty thousand, so the standard, map I had provided complete street guides not only to Lakeport but to all the other towns and villages of any size.

I checked the listing of Lakeport streets. Then I 'tried Lucerne, a little resort community on the northeast shore; nothing for me there either. Nice? Nice was a kind of sister hamlet to Lucerne, a few miles away and a bit smaller.

And there it was.

In Nice, high up off Lakeview Drive, was a short street that had the shape of a dog's leg on the map—a street called Thornapple Way.

I TOYED WITH THE IDEA of driving up to Lake County tonight, but it was a long way and the Cahill situation had left me physically and emotionally drained. Better to get as much rest as I could tonight and head out fresh in the morning.

So I took myself home. And there was a message from Kerry on the machine.

It was brief and it didn't say much: "Hi, babe. I'm sorry I

haven't called. I wanted to see you today but I have to go out again about two. Call me if you get in before that. Or tonight after six. We need to talk.'' I played it back three times. She sounded subdued but not grim or portentous. The ''hi, babe'' was a good sign; the ''we need to talk'' could be good or bad.

Six-fifteen now. I tapped out her number, but she wasn't home yet; her machine answered. After the beep I said, ''Just returning your call. I'm in for the evening—call or come on over.'' I hesitated, thought, What the hell, and said, ''Love you,'' before I disconnected.

I opened a can of minestrone, dumped in some grated Parmesan cheese, and cooked it up and ate it with a handful of crackers. It didn't set well, just seemed to lie simmering in my gullet while I sprawled out on the couch and listened to an old blues record. Bad choice of record, though: Bessie Smith singing such cheerful ballads as ''Down Hearted Blues'' and ''Down in the Dumps'' and ''Baby Have Pity on Me.'' I put a Pete Fountain tape on instead.

Seven o'clock.

I couldn't get my mind off Kerry. Memories . . . so damned many memories. The first time we'd made love, after she'd done most of the seducing. ''Ask me if I want to go to bed,'' she'd said, and I'd said, ''Do you want to go to bed?'' And she'd said, ''I thought you'd never ask,'' and took my hand and led me like a kid into my own bedroom. The way she'd looked and the way she'd-cried when I showed up at her door after the Deer Run nightmare. An afternoon we'd spent wandering among tide pools near Carmel. A night in a fancy motel in the Napa Valley, the two of us splashing like kids in one of those big in-room Jacuzzi tubs.

Other memories, too, not nearly so pleasant. Kerry saying, ''I think it would be better if we didn't see each other for a while,'' and then walking out of my old office on Drumm Street —the first time I thought I was losing her. And Kerry lying crumpled and bloody on the floor of my closet, not so long ago, beaten unconscious by a man who was after me . . .

Seven-thirty.

I got up and paced around, thinking: What a wreck I am. An old derelict floundering in heavy seas, looking for steerage back into a safe harbor.

The image that little metaphor conjured up made me laugh out loud. At myself, sardonically. An old derelict? A more apt description was of something darting around underwater, not floundering on top of it, something small and bright and silly: one of Walter Merchant's clownfish.

Eight o'clock, and eight-thirty, and nine.

I went in and took a hot bath. That usually starts the phone ringing off its hook, but not tonight. Out with Blessing again—where the hell else would she be? Driving me crazy. Down in the dumps. Baby, have pity on me.

But she didn't.

The phone stayed silent.

Chapter **20**

TAG END OF SUMMER in Lake County: hot, dry, the hills all brown and dusty and crawling with rattlesnakes, the hordes of vacationers and summer residents and beer-swilling youths thinning as the new school year approached—though at night they would still swarm as thickly as the mosquitoes and gnats. Lakeport and the other resort communities come alive in late May, thrive from mid-June to mid-September, and are done blooming by the first of October. The rest of the year—except for bass-fishing season, and year-round activities at Konocti Harbor Inn on the south shore—they're pretty much the domain of retirees, small business services, and vacation-industry people making preparations for next summer's influx.

I came in on Highway 20 from Ukiah, past Blue Lake and along the northern rim of Clear Lake. Even though it was Monday, traffic was heavy on the two-lane highway—slowed and clogged by cars and campers and behemoth motor homes and pickups towing boats. The midday heat was intense; I was simmering in my own sweat by the time I rolled into Nice.

At one time I'd driven up here once or twice a year, mostly

by myself, to fish for bass and catfish at Rodman Slough, midway between Nice and Lakeport. I remembered the last trip, four or five years ago. Eberhardt had come along and we'd rented a lakeside cabin in Lucerne. He'd caught two fat white cats the first morning, six pounders, and I'd caught some channel cats and a bullhead; we'd had fish fries three nights running, and drunk a couple of cases of beer each, and taken the rented boat all the way down to Jago Bay at the southern tip. We'd had a fine time . . . or at least I had. But when I'd suggested going back the following year, Eberhardt had backed out without much explanation.

Now, maybe, I knew why.

Damn the way things work out sometimes.

Nice hadn't changed much; I would have been surprised if it had. Lake County isn't affluent, and with the exception of small, upscale new communities at Soda Bay and Konocti Harbor, its resorts cater to young party animals and down-home middle-class adults who don't need fancy golf courses, tennis courts, and nightclubs to enjoy their summer vacations. Give them a small boat, a funky old tourist cabin, a good cheap restaurant, and a bar that has dancing to live country and western bands on weekends, and they're content. From what I knew of Nedra Merchant, she didn't fit into that down-home category—but then you never know about people. Maybe she had enough sophistication in the city and came up here for the change. Or maybe she hadn't come here of her own volition, back in May. Or maybe she'd never come here at all . . .

The village had the same unassuming, countrified look and feel that it had had forty years ago, the first time I'd visited here, and that it had probably had for decades before that. All that had been added recently were a few more houses on the steep folded hills rising inland from the lakeshore, at least one new restaurant and some junk shops masquerading as purveyors of antiques. If I'd been in a different mood, without so much weighing on my mind, I would have felt good coming back here. As it was, what I felt was relief that the long, hot trip was over.

Lakeview Drive hooked up off the main road; I turned there, wound my way along the lower reaches of the dry brown hills until I came to a sign that said Thornapple Way. It wasn't much of a street, just a two-block extension of asphalt that ran steeply up one side of a broad humpback. There were three houses on it, two down close to Lakeview Drive and the other atop the dogleg at the upper end, built into a notch in the hillside.

I drove up to the one in the notch: start at the top. No cars were parked at any of the three; the upper one had a garage, but it was closed and windowless. Nobody answered the bell there, or at either of the lower two. The middle one had its shutters up already, which no doubt meant the owners had closed it up and gone home. There were no names on mailboxes or anywhere else on the three properties.

Only one of the nearby houses on Lakeview Drive was occupied, by a thin middle-aged woman who didn't want to be bothered by somebody she didn't know on an errand she had no interest in. She had no idea who owned any of the houses on Thornapple Way, she said, which may or may not have been the truth. Ditto her claim, when I showed her the photo of Nedra Merchant, that she'd never seen the woman before. She minded her own business, she said, which was more than she could say for some people. Whereupon she shut her door in my face.

Friendly folk in the country. Or more likely, she was a city transplant who hadn't yet learned country ways and country manners and probably never would.

LAKEPORT HAD NOT CHANGED MUCH either. More people lived there—about a quarter of the county's population now—and its outskirts had expanded, in particular toward Kelseyville to the south. But its downtown area, along the lakefront, still had a pleasant old-fashioned atmosphere despite the noisy, garishly dressed and undressed summer people who clotted its streets, sidewalks, municipal park, and boat landing.

The hundred-year-old courthouse in the town square had been turned into a museum; the new courthouse, much larger and institutional-modern in design, rose up on the block behind it. I parked on Forbes Street and went into the new one. The county assessor's office was on the second floor. The woman clerk in there was polite and helpful; for a small fee she punched up the ownership records for the three houses on Thornapple Way.

Two of the names meant nothing to me. The third was Nedra Adams Merchant. She'd owned the property at number eight Thornapple Way a little less than two years, having had full title deeded over to her by the former owner. The purchase price had been twenty-five thousand dollars, a ridiculously low sum considering that the property's assessed value was five times that amount. The price didn't surprise me any more than the former owner's name.

The Liar, Dean Purchase.

SO NOW I HAD CONFIRMATION that Purchase had been mixed up big-time with Nedra Merchant. But the fact that he'd lied to me about that didn't necessarily mean he'd had anything to do with her disappearance. Or had any knowledge of the reasons behind it.

Was he involved or not? Had she come up here in May or not? Been living in her summer home all or part or none of the past three and a half months? Written and mailed those postcards to Dr. Muncon and Annette Olroyd? Was she here now, alive or dead?

I drove fast back around the northern rim of the lake. The answers to at least some of those questions were waiting for me at number eight Thornapple Way.

NUMBER EIGHT WAS THE UPPERMOST of the street's three houses, the one built into the notch atop the dogleg. It was a smallish place, narrow and two-storied, of a contemporary modular style that didn't blend in too well with the oaks and madrone and redbuds that flanked it. Its best feature was a terrace-size cedar deck that extended all along the ground-floor front and partway around on the far side. From out there you had a pan-

oramic view: all of Clear Lake, silvery blue under the hot midday
sun and loaded with boats and water skiers; the Mayacamas
Mountains to the west and the ragged jut of Cobb Mountain to
the south. The two-car garage was set apart from the house and
slightly above it. Past the garage and farther up the hillside, a
path led to a private picnic area shaded by huge heritage oaks.

I parked where I had earlier, in the short driveway that connected the garage to the street. It was quiet up here, a thick
midday hush broken only by a squalling jay and the faint drifting
whine of powerboats down on the lake. Heat hammered at me,
driving more sweat out of my pores. The summer smells of dust,
dry grass, tree spice, and lake water were so strong they made my
nostrils itch—and gave me a rush of childhood nostalgia that was
as powerful as a drug.

Over to the house first, to ring the bell again. Empty echoes
and no response. There was a rumpled screen door that opened
outward; I opened it and laid a hand on the inner door's knob. It
didn't yield when I turned it. I shut the screen, moved over to the
nearest window. Yellow twill drapes were pulled tight together
inside. I wandered around to the deck area on the south side. A
pair of sliding glass doors, another set of tight-drawn drapes.
Near the window was a Weber that hadn't been used in some
time: when I lifted the hood-shaped lid I found a rusted grill and
lots of spider silk. The rest of that section of deck was barren. So
was the long front part except for a couple of molded plastic
chairs.

I returned to the garage. It had a pair of manually operated
pull-up doors; both were secure. I circled the building. No other
doors and no windows. But it had been built of pine boards that
had begun to weather, and on the back side a gap had warped
open between two of the planks. On one, in the middle of the
gap, was a loose pine knot. I went and got the flashlight out of
the car. Back behind the garage, I used my Swiss Army knife to
pry out the loose knot and widen the gap. Then I laid the flashlight's lens at an angle next to the opening, switched it on, and
leaned close to squint one-eyed inside.

One car in there, an ice-blue color. I couldn't tell what it was at first, couldn't see any of the license plate. I fiddled around with the light and my angle of vision until more of the front end —and all of the hood ornament—came into view.

Mercedes. Fairly new, too, probably last year's model.

Nedra Merchant's car.

I MIGHT HAVE BEEN ABLE to pick one of the garage door locks, but it would have taken time and my chances of finding answers were better inside the house. The front door behind the screen had a dead-bolt lock on it; forget that. The adjacent window, also screened, had a simple catch lock, but the frame was down tight against the sill and there was no way I could wiggle a knife blade underneath to slip the catch. When I took a look at the sliding glass doors I saw that I couldn't get in through there either. Catch-locked, and judging from one door's refusal to budge even a little when I tugged on it, it was also fitted with a roller-bolt security lock at the bottom.

On the side nearest the garage were kitchen windows, at a level too high for me to see into. The sliding variety, screened on the outside. I stood for a few seconds, cleaning sweat off my face, scanning the area. A car drifted past on Lakeview Drive and disappeared; out of sight the other way, somebody began using a noisy leaf blower or chain saw. Otherwise, I seemed to have this portion of the hillside to myself. Dusty oaks and limp-looking redbuds grew densely on the far side of Thornapple Way—an effective screen between me and the houses beyond. Higher up, there was nothing except power lines and a long crease where two ground folds met that was choked with brush and deadfall, a fire hazard that ought to have been cleaned out.

Some cordwood was stacked against the garage wall. I poked among it until I found a thick, unsplit chunk about two feet long. Back to the house, where I wedged the log down under the kitchen windows. When I climbed up on top of it I could rest my arms on the narrow sill and look inside past frilly yellow-and-white curtains. Not that there was anything to see except a standard bare-bones kitchen.

I gave my attention to the windows. They were locked, but the catch didn't look like much: the weakest security point in a high percentage of homes, old and new, is the kitchen windows. The screen popped out with one tug; I lifted it down. Then I went to work on the window catch with my knife and brute force.

When the thing finally gave under a hard yank, I lost my balance and fell sideways off the log and banged my knee, bruised my thigh on the flashlight I'd tucked into my pants pocket. I did some cussing, feeling clumsy and foolish. Damn me for the big clown I was! I picked myself up and hobbled around until the pain subsided. The flashlight hadn't been damaged, small miracle. I clipped it to my belt in back, which is what I should have done in the first place.

I righted the log, climbed onto it again. Slid the window open as far as it would go. The opening looked wide enough for me to wiggle through. Another check of my surroundings, and up I went, using my forearms for leverage, shoes scrabbling against the wall. It took me more than a minute to haul my body through and get a foot anchored on the sink drainboard.

In getting the foot down I dislodged a plate and a glass, sent them toppling to shatter on the floor. The plate and glass were dirty, recently dirty: bits of food and some kind of brownish liquid flew up with the shards. More dishes were stacked on the drainboard and in the sink; those, too, had been used not so long ago. By Nedra Merchant? Or by somebody else?

I swung down to the floor, took a closer look at the dishes. No residue of lipstick or anything else that might tell me the user's gender or identity. Or whether one person or two or more had eaten off them.

Through an open doorway I could see the front hall and part of the staircase to the upper floor. I headed that way. Closed up as it was, the place was stifling; I had trouble taking in the dust-clogged air. Across the hall, the living room waited in shadowed neatness. More of Nedra Merchant's poster-work adorned the walls in there, but otherwise the room contained nothing of hers. The furniture was of good quality, but it ran to leather and dark wood: Dean Purchase's taste, not hers. Either she hadn't gotten around to replacing it or she liked it as it was.

Dripping sweat, I climbed the stairs and prowled through the two bedrooms and bathroom on the upper level. One bedroom hadn't been used in a long while; the other had been occupied as recently as last night. The double bed in that one was rumpled, the bottom sheet pulled half off the mattress, the upper sheet and a light blanket wadded at the foot. There was a stain of some kind on the bottom sheet. . . . Christ, semen?

On the floor next to the bed, its lid raised, sat a Gucci suitcase—either a part of the set of luggage in the storeroom at Nedra's city house, or a twin. The case was three-quarters full of light summer clothing, all in the bright colors and Oriental style she favored; there was also some lingerie. Newly arrived and not yet completely unpacked? Or getting ready to leave and not yet completely packed? I couldn't tell which.

The closet held a few more of her summer things, plus a man's robe and a man's silk aloha shirt—both of medium size. Shoes, a spare purse . . . otherwise the cupboard was bare. Nothing in the dresser other than a couple of skimpy swimsuits. And nothing on or in either of the nightstands.

The bathroom was another bust. So was the downstairs toilet. In the kitchen again, I opened the refrigerator. Bread, milk, cold cuts and cheese, a carton half full of deli potato salad—all fresh, no more than a couple of days old. Two bottles of dark stout, a jar of mustard, another of green olives. In the freezer compartment, a pint container of Häagen-Dazs rum-raisin ice cream with one small scoop out of it.

When I shut the freezer door the leaf blower or chain saw noise from downhill quit abruptly, and the silence in there turned as thick and clotted as the trapped heat. Or did it? I thought I heard something—faint, faraway, inside rather than outside the house. But when I stood rigid and strained to listen, I couldn't identify it or its source. Maybe if I shut the window . . . I reached up and slid it closed, listened again.

Now I was sure I heard something. A kind of humming, fluttery sound. Refrigerator motor? No, it wasn't like that. It was like . . . a fan going somewhere, a small electric fan.

But if a fan was running in here, I couldn't figure where. I'd been through every room in the house—

That door in the back wall, next to the stove. Where did that lead?

I'd noticed the door earlier, but I hadn't really paid much attention to it. Kitchens have doors to pantries, storage closets; you take them for granted, don't focus on them unless you have a reason to. Now I had a reason. And the first thing I saw when I got close to this door was that it was outfitted with a new-looking Schlage knob-and-lock plate, and an equally new-looking eyebolt lock mounted above.

Why lock a pantry? Why put *two* locks on a pantry door?

I pressed my ear against the heavy wood panel. The fluttery hum was coming from the other side—definitely some kind of electric fan. I worked the eyebolt free of its hasp, slid it back. But the key lock below had been turned and it was a dead-bolt, not the kind you can pop with a knife blade or credit card. Dead-bolt locks are also damned hard to pick, even by somebody with professional or semiprofessional skills.

Key might be here somewhere, I thought.

It was, but I almost missed it. I opened drawers, cabinets, the doors under the sink . . . and the whole time it was hanging in plain sight from a hook screwed into the wall next to the refrigerator. "Get your eyesight checked," I muttered aloud, and took the key off the hook and unlocked the door.

It opened inward into heavy blackness. The fan sound was loud now and I could feel the breeze from it. The air was cooler in there but still sluggish—and rank with smells that closed my throat, made my stomach dance. Dry earth and must, soiled clothing, body odor and body waste. Instinctively I wanted to back up, get away from the stench and what was hidden by the dark. Instead I dragged the flashlight off my belt, fumbled for the switch.

Something stirred in the darkness.

Something made a whimpering noise.

Something said in a cracked voice that made my skin crawl, "Baby? Please let me come out, Baby. Please don't make me stay in here anymore. Baby? Please, Baby, I'll be good to you."

I clicked on the flash.

The light pinned her, and she made the whimpering noise again and flung an arm up in front of her face. I made a sound, too, when I saw her. She was crouched on all fours, wearing nothing but bra and panties, her hair hanging down and shiny black in the glare. But it was her face, her eyes that tore the sound out of me. Jesus, her eyes . . .

"Baby?"

I had found Nedra Merchant—what was left of her.

Chapter 21

I TOOK THE LIGHT OFF HER, swept it around. Grotesque shadows capered over wood and stone and packed earth; an object gleamed in one corner like a creature with a huge dead eye. Overhead, the beam picked up a low-wattage bulb suspended from a rafter, a piece of string dangling below it. I moved ahead, caught hold of the string and yanked. Most of the dark disintegrated under a burst of dim yellow.

It was like a cave in there. Or an animal's lair.

Or a prison cell.

The part just inside the door had once been a pantry about six feet deep. Shelves covered the bare-wood walls on both sides, some bearing a small cache of canned goods; the lower section of one shelf had been torn down, torn apart, its broken pieces since picked up and stacked neatly to one side. You could see where a wall and another door had enclosed the rear of the pantry: the vertical beams and hinges were still there. The rest of the construction had been removed to open up the part where the woman was, where I now stood.

That part was maybe ten feet square, with a low, sloping

ceiling that was no more than six feet high at the far end; lime-
stone walls shored up by thick crossbeams and a floor that was
partly packed earth and partly bare rock. Root cellar. Houses in
this section of the state, those built into hillside notches like this
one, still had them; they made for relatively cool storage places
in the hot climate. A hole had been bored through the rock from
under the house and a length of one-inch PVC pipe inserted
through it—probably for ventilation purposes. A four-outlet extension cord ran in here from a wall plug in the pantry; the fan
was plugged into that. So was the object that had gleamed like a
dead eye: a small TV set. The rest of the space was cramped with
a rollaway bed, a rocking chair, a portable camper's toilet, and a
table piled high with magazines and artist's tools—sketchpads,
pencils, paints.

Nedra Merchant was crouched on the bed, her hands covering her eyes now—the posture of a child. Her fingers were cut
and torn, two of the nails ripped completely off, all painted now
with iodine. She'd tried to batter her way out with shelf wood,
dig her way out with her bare hands: there was a pathetically
small hole in the earth along one wall. She was stick-figure thin,
her ribs showing, bones jutting against dead-white skin, her
cheeks and eyes deeply sunken as if all the flesh were rotting
away. Her hair was clean, washed within the past couple of days,
and she'd been put in here with a fresh white dress that she'd
taken off and thrown on the floor, and she wore lipstick that
made her mouth look like a bloody wound. All prettied up and
waiting for Baby.

The wound opened and words came out. "Turn off the light,
Baby. It's better in the dark."

"Open your eyes, Nedra. Look at me."

The unfamiliar voice brought her hands down; she blinked
several times, peered at me through slits—and then shrank back
hard against the wall. "You're not Baby," she said in a whimper.

"Who is? Who did this to you?"

"I don't know you. What are you doing here?"

"I'm a friend. I came to help—"

"No. Where's Baby? I want Baby."

Looking at her, listening to her, had unleashed a storm of emotions in me—rage, compassion, a sickening remembered dread. It was as if I were back in that frigging Deer Run cabin, looking at myself after all those days I'd been chained to the wall, seeing myself as I would have looked if I hadn't been strong enough, if my ordeal had broken me as Nedra Merchant's had broken her. The parallel was terrifying. I had come away scarred but whole. Nedra Merchant was going to come away in pieces that all the king's horses and all the king's men might never put together again.

How long had she held out? A week, a month, two months, longer? Fighting until she couldn't fight anymore, and then . . . what? Had she gone over the edge clawing and screaming or had she just let go? One thing for sure: When she'd landed it had been in a place that submerged her fear, turned hatred for her jailer into clinging need. In that soft, twisted place he had stopped being her tormentor and become her protector, the only person who could save her and set her free.

I wanted to kill him for what he had done to her, just as I had wanted to kill the man who imprisoned me. Nobody, no matter who she'd been or what she'd done in her life, should have to suffer the way Nedra had; the person responsible deserved to die for it. The impulse was so strong in me I began to shake. I had to take a double grip on the flashlight, clutch it tight against my chest to keep my hands still. The bloodlust, and the heat and the foul air, brought on a dizziness, a churning in my stomach. I needed to get myself out of here almost as much as I needed to get her out.

I moved toward her. Doing it slowly so I wouldn't frighten her any more than she already was. But she scrambled backward anyway, came off the bed onto her feet. "No! Stay away from me; don't come near me!"

"I won't hurt you, Nedra."

"Stay away!"

"I swear I won't, I only want to help you . . ."

I kept on crooning to her, gently, moving all the while. She hugged the wall, crouched and motionless, until I was within two steps of her; then she yelled, shrill and wild, and flung herself at me with her hands hooked into claws.

Even as emaciated as she was, she had a maniacal strength. I dropped the torch and caught her wrists, but I couldn't hold her. Broken nails raked across my neck; she brought up a knee that I turned away from just in time, took on my upper thigh. I drove her backward with my body, pinned her against the rock, got her arms locked down at her sides. She went right on twisting and straining against me, all boneless sinew and muscle, like a cat struggling for release.

"You're safe now, Nedra, it's all right, you're safe. . . ."

She spit in my face, twice; screeched obscenities in my ear. I went on crooning in a soft monotone. The soothing quality of my voice, if not what I was saying, got through to her; or maybe she just ran out of breath and strength. The obscenities trickled off into little mewlings, and her struggles grew feeble, and finally she sagged limply in my grasp.

I relaxed my hold a little, to find out if she was shamming. She wasn't. I backed up, taking her with me; let go of her wrist and slid my arm up and around her shoulders and turned her toward the door. She came along all right, muttering something under her breath—the same words over and over, as if she were reciting some kind of lesson.

"I don't care, I don't care, I don't care. . . ."

I walked her into the pantry section, into the open doorway to the kitchen. There was sweat in my eyes from all the exertion, impairing my vision like rainwater on window glass; I couldn't wipe it away because of my grip on Nedra. I saw movement on my right as we passed through the doorway, but indistinctly, and when I turned that way, blinking, she came alive in my arms.

She brought her heel down hard on my instep, emitting the shrill cry again, and then tore loose. I clutched at her, missed— and something hit me from the side, high up across the bridge of my nose. My vision went completely cockeyed. A second blow, hard on my left temple, thrust me backward; my feet slid out from under me and I went down, banging my head against one of the shelves.

I lost consciousness. Not for long—a clutch of seconds, no more than a minute. All at once, then, I was aware of a ringing in my ears, of pain. And then I was up on one knee, shaking my head, pawing at my eyes.

When I could see again I was looking at the door to the kitchen. It was closed now, shut tight. I heaved to my feet, stumbled to it, twisted the knob and shook the door; it wouldn't open, wouldn't open—

Baby had come back. And Baby had Nedra again.

And now I was locked in this hellhole in her place.

THE CLAUSTROPHOBIA STARTED immediately, building fast, spiraling into raw terror. I started to shake again, a violent trembling like an old structure in an earthquake—shaking itself apart from the inside out.

Don't panic!

I told myself that over and over, leaning against the door, but the part of me where the terror lived refused to listen. Curb the panic or it would cripple me, turn me into the same gibbering thing Nedra had become.

Off the wall, turn around—movements that brought sharp surges of pain in my head, face, leg. Pain, I thought. And I was seeing the boards from the torn-down shelf stacked against the wall. And in the next second, or what seemed like the next second, I had one of the boards in my hand and was swinging it like a baseball bat against my sore left knee.

I swung it again, then a third time, with as much force as I could muster. On the third blow the leg buckled and I was back on the floor. By then the pain was high and hot in my knee and inside my head—a fire that consumed the terror, reduced it to glowing ashes.

I sat there trying to get my breath, waiting for the fire to burn itself out. It took a minute or two, and at the end of that time I could think clearly again: I was back in control.

The first time I tried to stand, my left leg wouldn't support me and I collapsed. I'd cut the knee up with the board; my pant leg was torn and there was a bloody gash that ran two inches down from the kneecap. No swelling though. Sweat stung my eyes, in a bleeding cut on my forehead, in the furrows left by Nedra's nails; the hand I swiped across my face came away smeared with a mixture of water and blood. I rested for a minute or so, massaging the knee, before I shoved upright for another try. This time, when I put weight on the leg, it held me.

Agony on the first few steps. Then that pain began to fade as I slow-paced back and forth between the pantry and the end of the cellar. Eight, nine, ten times I retraced my steps, until I could walk more or less normally again.

By then I was aware of every inch of that damned cell, of everything in it. Evil place . . . but it wasn't escape-proof. It was not an isolated cabin in the wilderness, I was not chained to a wall, that locked door was not impregnable. There were tools at my disposal. I could get out of here. I *would* get out of here—and soon, long before any of my own private demons came raging back.

I bent to examine the door. I'd left the key in the lock on the kitchen side; all he'd had to do was turn it. Had he thrown the eyebolt too? I yanked on the knob, up and down, back and forth. Maybe not. There was some give, more than there would be if the door were double-locked into the jamb. Good, fine. I had my Swiss Army knife, with its multitude of blades and gadgets; and the wood of the jamb was old and relatively soft, scarred by deep gouges where Nedra Merchant had dug at it with some kind of makeshift tool. I could work on it until I exposed the bolt, then pry or break it loose. But that would take hours, possibly even a full day, and I did not have that much time to spare; I'd come apart for sure.

Had to be another way, a quicker way . . .

I pawed among the cans on the shelves. Cans were all there

was . . . no help there. I walked back into the cellar; except for
a faint dull ache, my knee gave me no trouble. Nothing I could
do with the toilet or fan or TV set or rocking chair. The table? As
a battering ram? It looked solid, but when I swept off the artist's
supplies and picked it up, I saw that it wasn't solid at all. One
good bang against a hard surface and it would break up into
kindling.

The bed?

I got down on my good knee next to it for a close look. It
wasn't new and it didn't appear to be very sturdy; I remembered
creaking sounds when Nedra moved on it. But the two long and
two short sections of the frame were made of forged steel. Seeing
that gave me an idea, one that might work if I could get the frame
apart.

I stripped off the mattress and box spring, then lifted the
frame up onto its side so I could tell how the corners had been
joined. Riveted and spot-welded, the stubby castered feet attached the same way. Cheaply made, too; rust spots speckled the
metal and I could feel the give when I put pressure on one corner. I took a tight grip on the thing and banged it down hard on
the bottom corner, driving it into the bare rock where the cellar
floor met the wall.

But getting the rivets and weld to snap wasn't as easy as I
had hoped. There wasn't much room to maneuver and I kept
having to stop and dry my slick hands. The exertion, combined
with the heat and the stink, brought back the sick, dizzy feeling. I
remembered the fan and moved it over to where it would blow on
my face. That helped a little. Helped keep my hands drier too.

I worked in a steady, mindless rhythm: any kind of thinking
would only have gotten in the way. It might have been ten minutes and it might have been half an hour before the one joint
finally broke apart. I tried standing on one of the longer sections
and using brute force to tear it free at the other corner. The strain
weakened the joining but didn't snap it. To do that I had to turn
the frame over and continually beat the corner against rock, as I
had the opposite one.

Another ten or fifteen or twenty minutes . . . and the frame split into a pair of uneven right angles. I took one of them to the door, wedged the short piece under the knob against the casing, with the long piece angled down to the floor. Fulcrum, pry bar. Bent forward at the waist, with my legs spread, I locked hands under the lower end, lifted, then heaved upward against the knob with all the strength in my upper body. Once, twice, three times. The effort left me panting. I wiped my face, dried my hands, took another grip and tried again.

This time the wood above the knob began to wrinkle.

Lift, heave. Lift, heave . . . driving upward with my legs, grunting like Hulk Hogan. Blood-pound in my ears, tearing sensation across my shoulders. And lift, heave—

The knob bent, the wood around it splintered.

One more heave and the knob snapped, throwing me off-balance. I lost my grip on the section of bed frame and it dropped clattering, barked one of my shins on the rebound.

I righted myself against the shelves. Picked up the frame, backed off, drove the short piece against the casing. The eyebolt *hadn't* been thrown; the door popped open as soon as the Schlage dead bolt tore loose on my second thrust. I threw the frame away behind me, kicked the door the rest of the way open, and staggered out into the kitchen.

There was so much blood and sweat in my eyes I was nearly blind. I groped across to the sink, ran cold water, and put my head under the stream until my vision was clear and the heat flush on my face eased. I dried off with a towel from a wall rack; the still-bleeding cut on my forehead stained the towel red. Then I leaned on the drainboard to wait for my pulse rate to slow, some of the tension and the last vestiges of the claustrophobia to drain away.

I'd banged my watch a few times while I was working in there, but the second hand still rotated on the dial. Good old Timex—takes a licking and keeps on ticking. The time surprised me: not even four o'clock yet. As impossible as it seemed, I had been trapped less than an hour.

Through the window I could see my car parked in front of the garage—the only car out there. They were long gone. But I did not feel any real urgency, not anymore.

I knew who Baby was; I'd known it from the moment I laid eyes on Nedra Merchant in her prison.

And I knew where he would take her from here.

Chapter **22**

ON THE WAY OUT OF NICE I had a wrangle with myself. Call the county sheriff? Baby and Nedra would be out of Lake County by now, and the law up here was not going to put out a pickup order on my say-so, not unless I came in and showed ID and told my story in person. Call the SFPD? Branislaus had had weekend duty, which meant he wouldn't be working today; I'd have to talk to another inspector, fill him in, try to convince him to make this a priority matter—and by the time they acted, Baby and Nedra would be at their destination. So would I, probably. Besides, if the cops came bulling in on them, there was no telling what he might do. He hadn't harmed her directly and he wouldn't as long as there was no provocation, but if officers with guns and bull-horns showed up . . . No, this was a situation better handled by me alone, one on one. Time was on my side too: I was only about an hour behind them, and if I got lucky, drove faster than he did, I might be able to cut the gap down to half an hour or so.

I got half lucky. Traffic heading west on Highway 20 was fairly light once I passed Upper Lake, and I was able to make pretty good time except for a two-mile snag behind a slow-moving camper. It was just five o'clock when I reached the junction with 101 above Ukiah. On the freeway I opened up to seventy, to seventy-five on the straighter stretches; I was afraid to risk any higher speeds. If a highway patrolman stopped me, I would have to sit still for questions and maybe some hassle. Before leaving the Thornapple house I'd taken an antiseptic bandage from the first-aid kit in the trunk and covered the cut on my forehead, but my face was still beat-up and my neck bore the marks of Nedra's nails. Any cop would take one close look at me and become suspicious as hell.

I made good time until I neared Santa Rosa. Then I ran into an accident jam, and by the time I got past the blocked lane on the south side of town, I'd lost most of the twenty minutes or so I'd gained early on. Sometimes when you roll the dice you come up with snake eyes.

It was six forty-five when I crossed the Golden Gate Bridge, and after seven when I reached Forest Hill. They were there, all right; his car was parked in front of the red-shingled garage. I stopped across the street. The only firearm I own, a lightweight .38 Smith & Wesson Bodyguard, I keep clipped under the dash; I popped it free, put it into the pocket of my jacket, then donned the jacket as I got out.

The gate in front of the house was shut. I still had Runyon's key but I did not want to go in the front way if I could help it. I detoured to the side stairway, descended slowly to the landing midway down the hillside. The storeroom door was recessed under an overhang there.

The key worked that lock as well as the ones on the gate and the front entrance. I eased the door open, myself inside; shut it behind me. Stood listening until my eyes adjusted to the gloom and I could see the way across to the interior door. There were no sounds to hear.

I picked my way through the storeroom, peered into the downstairs hall. More empty silence. Wherever they were and whatever they were doing, they were being quiet about it. I entered the hall, moving quickly now that I had carpet underfoot, and poked my head around the doorway into the master bedroom. They weren't in there, which was a small relief. It would have been bad, walking in on them having sex; I don't know what I would have done. Consensual abuse is still abuse, the more so in Nedra Merchant's case.

I padded down to her office and the spare bedroom; they were also empty. Back to the stairs . . . and above, not far away, I heard somebody cough. It didn't sound right—liquidy, strangulated, the cough of a person in pain.

I went up fast to the middle landing, where the upper half of the stairs turned back in the opposite direction. A decorative wrought-iron banister ran partway around the staircase and through the pickets I could see into the entrance hall. What was up there made me stop, put a fresh clutch of tension across my shoulders. It also knocked me mentally off-balance, because it was not at all what I'd expected to find here.

He was sitting on the floor, his back against the wall facing me, his feet splayed out in front of him. Blood, a lot of it, had dyed the front of his pale-blue shirt a glistening crimson. His eyes were squeezed tightly shut and I couldn't tell if he was breathing . . . until his chest heaved and another cough, then a ragged series of coughs, racked his body. The floor around him was littered with objects: two large plastic bags that evidently had been dropped, spilling their contents. Cosmetics, perfumes, two small gift-wrapped packages, a bottle of champagne, several food items. On its side half in and half out of the bathroom doorway, as if it had been dropped or kicked there, was a suitcase —Nedra's suitcase, the one that I'd seen in the bedroom at the Thornapple house.

I climbed up the rest of the way, cautiously, with my gaze swiveling between the formal living room on my right and the kitchen straight ahead. Nothing and nobody to see in either place. I went into the kitchen, then the family room; looked out onto the deck; checked the attached garage and the bathroom. Nedra wasn't here. Nobody was here except Baby.

I knelt beside him. The wound in his chest was down low,

under the right breast. Maybe life-threatening, maybe not; he'd lost a half pint of blood and it depended on the angle of penetration and where the bullet had lodged. Shot with a small-caliber handgun—probably a .22. There was no sign of the weapon among the litter on the floor.

It must have been Nedra, I thought. . . . But then where was she and where was the gun? I could see her shooting him, if she'd somehow thrown off her psychological dependency and acted in a rush of hatred. But I couldn't see her doing it and then charging out of the house on foot with the weapon in her hand. He'd turned her into a burrow animal, and animals don't run wild in the daylight when they're hurt. They hide in the dark and lick their wounds.

Whoever did it, I thought, it's partly my fault. If I'd called the SFPD from Nice, this wouldn't have happened. Then I thought: No, damn it, you don't know that's so. Explanations, priorities . . . the cops might not have gotten here any faster than you did. Some of the fault is Nedra's and most of it is Baby's; none of it is yours.

He coughed again, then started to shiver. I hurried downstairs and got a blanket out of the master bedroom and brought it up and put it around him. It didn't stop the shivering. I leaned down and said against his ear, "Who did this to you?" His eyes stayed shut and he didn't answer. He was conscious—wheezing with his mouth open, licking at cracked lips with a liverish tongue—but his awareness was a small, shriveled thing huddled somewhere in the dark within.

Seeing him like this, I felt nothing for him except the thin, detached pity I would have felt for any gunshot victim. No rage, no compassion, no sense of sorrow. Every man has demons and he'd let his destroy him, nearly destroy several innocent people; I had no patience with a man like that, no room inside me for understanding and forgiveness. I reserved my feelings for the fighters, the bogey-bashers and demon-slayers, the selfless ones who might hurt themselves but could never be driven to harm others.

The front door was locked; I opened it and took a quick look at the latch. No scratches, no marks of any kind. Then I went back into the family room. Something in there had caught my eye on the first pass: a glass on the coffee table where Runyon's flower shrine had sat. It was a tall glass, half full of a dark liquid that was probably bourbon and three melting ice cubes.

Right.

From the phone in there I called 911, told the dispatcher who answered that I had a gunshot emergency and needed an ambulance right away at 770 Crestmont. She asked my name, and I hesitated and then disconnected without giving it to her. It wasn't the smartest move, to walk away from the scene of a shooting, especially if one of the neighbors happened to see me doing it. But I couldn't bear the thought of hanging around here, waiting, going through another endless Q. & A. session. I had a pretty good idea now of where Nedra was and who had shot Baby. And I could do something about it if I got out of here immediately.

He was still sitting as I'd left him, still wheezing, still licking his dry lips. I went past him, opened the door again. There were no sirens yet, but it wouldn't be long before an ambulance and a police cruiser or two came shrieking up the hill. Gunshot emergency response in the city is usually fast . . . in upper middle-class white neighborhoods like this one anyway.

Leaving the door open, I crossed the deck and cracked the gate. The street was empty and there were no pedestrians. To make things as easy as possible for the cops and the paramedics, I left the gate ajar too.

It was the last thing I could or would do for Victor Runyon.

DOWNHILL ON IRVING I stopped at a service station that had a public telephone booth with a still-usable directory. The address I wanted was listed, a number on Paraiso Place. I had to look up Paraiso on my city map: a short street in the Parkside District, between Sloat Boulevard and Stern Grove. Fairly close to where I was now; ten or fifteen minutes, depending on traffic.

As I drove out Nineteenth, my head was full of Victor Runyon. What had happened between him and Nedra, beginning in early May, was not hard to figure now. He had been coming apart slowly for some time: years of overwork and stress, the added stress of his affair with Nedra. She had been the catalyst, and the final catalytic act was her ending their relationship. That was what turned her from the controller into the controlled; from the predator into the victim.

Angry words, threats, at her home on Saturday, May 9th; an ugly scene. That day, or the next, Nedra had driven up to Lake County—to get away from Runyon, or maybe just to be alone for a while. When he found her gone he figured out where she went and drove to Nice himself. Another confrontation, even more volatile, and the last threads of his sanity had unraveled. He'd locked her in the root cellar. Not with any intention of keeping her there, not at first; just a wild and angry attempt to force her into changing her mind. But she had spirit and she'd made the mistake of resisting him, taunting or threatening him. A day or two or three, and by then it was too late: he was committed. He'd hold her prisoner until she saw things his way, agreed to marry him. An impossible fantasy, but in his battered mind it was his only hope.

It wouldn't have been difficult for Runyon, an architect, to turn that cellar into a livable cell, no more than a couple of days' work with her locked in the downstairs toilet where she could yell her head off without being heard. He'd have had the .22 with him by then, to keep her obedient. Early May was when he'd taken the gun from his garage, not last Saturday. I'd have bet money on it.

Before too long, Nedra would have stopped openly fighting him, pretended to give in, said or done anything to free herself. But she'd have waited too long: he didn't believe her. Hate and malice had gotten mixed up with his desperate love; he'd wanted to punish her as well as bend her to his will. Three and a half months . . . he'd punished her, all right. Broken her at last. He must have realized that when he went up there again on Saturday, and it was a good thing for her that he had. Otherwise she'd be dead now. They both would be.

Runyon had reached the point of killing himself; the good-bye letter to his wife proved that. But suicide wasn't the only thing on his mind when he walked out of his house Saturday evening. If Nedra had continued to resist him in any way, or if he'd still felt there was no hope for the two of them, he'd have shot her before turning the .22 on himself. I'd have bet money on that too.

Instead he'd found a totally dependent Nedra, all his at last. "Baby," she'd said, and he'd taken her out of her prison, and cleaned her up, and made love to her, and yesterday or this morning he'd packed her bag and promised to take her home. Today he'd locked her up again—"just for a little while," he'd have said to her—while he ran around Lakeport buying her cosmetics, presents, food, and champagne to celebrate their homecoming. Even finding me there with her hadn't changed his plans. All he cared about was the two of them, being together, going home.

It all seemed so clear-cut . . . and yet I hadn't tumbled to any of it, hadn't had a glimmer of suspicion, until I saw Nedra crouching inside her prison. No one had suspected—except, for God's sake, Eddie Cahill. Had Runyon let something slip in one of his monologues at the Crestmont house that Cahill had over-heard? Or was his belief in Runyon's guilt based on reasoning as wrongheaded and monomaniacal as Runyon's? Didn't matter much, either way. The point was, that damned shrine had acted like a screen to obscure the truth from me; so had the things Runyon had told me on the way to S. F. General, the things he'd done to preserve Nedra's home and finances. They were all part of a madness much deeper and more complex than a layman like me could have diagnosed. His lies were not so much calculated falsehoods as self-denials of the terrible act he'd committed. The shrine, the paying of her bills, the preservation of her mail and her phone messages, were not just expressions of blind, sick faith; they were devotional preparations for her homecoming, the beginning of their life together.

Still, even with all the complexity and obfuscations, I might have guessed at least some of the truth. There were things that pointed to it, like lights in a heavy fog. Kay Runyon had told me her husband traveled a lot as part of his profession, that he'd increased his travel time considerably over the past several months. If I'd checked into that I'd have discovered that few if any of his recent trips were business-related. When he'd left the city it had been to go to Lake County, to attend to Nedra. Then there were the postcards. As far as I knew, only two people had received cards—Dr. Muncon and Annette Olroyd, the only two who had expressed serious concern in messages left on her answering machine. Runyon had monitored those tapes; he'd told me so himself. The only other person who had listened to them was me.

And finally there were things he'd said on the ride to the hospital, revealing little phrases. *Give it enough time, she'll change her mind. I know she will. She* has *to.* And: *I do know she's alive, she's all right, she's not really hurt.* And: *[I'm her] lover and best friend. Now especially she needs no one but me.* And: *She'll come back, safe and sound. She has to, for both our sakes. You understand? She'll come back with me.* That last was the most telling of all. *With me,* he'd said, not *to me.* I just hadn't paid attention to the word choice at the time.

THE HOUSE ON PARAISO PLACE was small and Spanish-style: white stucco, red tile roof, wrought-iron trim. In front was a pocket-size lawn and a couple of cypress that had been sculpted to resemble bonsai trees. In the driveway alongside sat a new beige Cadillac Eldorado. Maybe that was a good sign and maybe it wasn't. I would have liked it better if Walter Merchant weren't home, if he'd taken Nedra straight to a hospital.

I parked behind the Caddy, went up and laid into the bell. When I finally let up I thought I heard steps inside, but the door didn't open. I leaned on the bell some more, kept it up for a full minute. The door stayed shut.

''The hell with this,'' I said aloud. Then, in a much louder voice, I called out my name and: "I know you're in there, Merchant. Open up, damn it, and talk to me."

Nothing at first. But as I was about to sing out again, he said from close behind the door, "Go away. We don't have anything to talk about."

"Don't play games with me. I just came from Nedra's house. I called the paramedics but not the police, not yet. You've got ten seconds before I do. And you won't like what I tell them."

He used all ten seconds to make up his mind. A chain rattled, the door swung inward. Walter Merchant didn't look like a confident, dignified, take-charge lawyer tonight. He was pale, slump-shouldered, his hair mussed, his clothing rumpled and untucked. There was a hunted look in his eyes. And across the front of his pin-striped shirt, smears of dried blood.

He said dully, "How did you know to come here?"

"Lucky guess." But it hadn't been. He'd told me in his office that he hadn't given Nedra any reason to change the locks on her house after the divorce; that being the case, and given his feelings for her, it was reasonable to assume he'd kept a key, just in case. And he'd been hanging around there on Saturday night, with his torch for her burning hot. And who else but Merchant would have made himself a drink in there tonight, made himself at home in the place that used to be his home?

I pushed past him, into a living room furnished expensively but without much style or taste. There was nobody in it except Merchant and another collection of tropical fish in a tank that matched the one in his office.

"Where's Nedra?"

"In the bedroom. I put her to bed."

"Why didn't you take her to a hospital?"

"I was going to, but . . . I wasn't thinking clearly, I didn't have any idea what had happened to her. I still don't, except that she's been through some kind of hell. . . ."

"The worst kind."

"What did he do to her, for God's sake?"

"Locked her in a root cellar in a house she owns in Lake County. That's where she's been the whole three and a half months."

"Jesus!"

"How did you get her here?" I asked him. "She wouldn't have come willingly, not the shape she's in."

"She was . . . wild. She didn't even seem to know me at first. I couldn't control her, she tried to claw me. . . . I had to hit her and then carry her to the car." A tremor ran through him at the memory. "I never hit her while we were married. Never, not once."

"She still unconscious?"

"She woke up when we got here. She knew me then— didn't try to fight me anymore. She was . . . God, it was like she was a zombie. I had some sleeping pills, I got her into bed and made her take one. . . ."

"Show me where she is."

He led me into a shadowed bedroom at the rear. Nedra was asleep on her back, with a comforter tucked up under her chin. Her gaunt, bloodless face didn't look quite so ravaged in repose. I went over and listened to her breathing. It sounded normal enough.

"That bruise on her chin," Merchant said miserably. "That's where I hit her."

I had nothing to say to that. I took hold of his arm, prodded him out of there and back into the living room.

"What happened with Runyon?" I asked then.

"Runyon. Is that his name?"

"You never saw him before?"

"No, he was a stranger to me. Is he dead?"

"No."

"But he's badly hurt? He might die?"

"He might, but I doubt it."

"That's too bad. I wish I'd killed the son of a bitch."

"No you don't. You're a lawyer, Merchant; you know better than that."

He drew a deep, shaky breath, started to speak, changed his mind, and sank bonelessly onto the arm of a leather couch. Pretty soon he said, "I was in the house when they walked in. I don't know why I went there again tonight. The same perverse impulse that made me drive by on Saturday, I guess. I'd been thinking about her all day, I couldn't get her out of my mind."

"What happened when they came in?"

"As soon as I saw her—the way she looked—I went a little crazy. He had his arm around her and I tried to pull her away. She screamed, tried to jump on me, and he pulled his damn gun and waved it in my face. . . . I don't know, I tried to take it away from him and he . . . it went off. The muzzle must have been right up against his body."

"All right," I said.

"I felt him jerk and then he fell down and Nedra . . . that's when she tried to claw me, that's when I hit her. I hated to, but . . . the only way I could stop her—"

"Where's the gun?"

". . . What?"

"The gun. It wasn't in the hallway with Runyon. You must have taken it with you."

Blank stare. "I don't remember."

"Were you wearing a coat or jacket?"

"Suit jacket."

"Where is it?"

"I must have taken it off, but I don't remember where."

I left him and went hunting through the house. He'd shed the jacket in the bathroom adjacent to the room where Nedra was sleeping. The .22 was jammed into one of the pockets. The front sight had ripped through the cloth and it was hung up in there; I had to tear the pocket even more to get it free. I wrapped the weapon in a towel, took it out to the living room.

Merchant looked at the bundle, shook his head and looked at me. He said, "What do we do now?"

"One of us is going to call nine-eleven," I said, "and get an ambulance out here for Nedra. Then one of us is going to notify the police, tell them what happened to Victor Runyon. It'll be a lot better for all concerned—you in particular—if you're the one who makes both calls.''

"Yes. You're right.'' He shoved off the couch arm, started across to where a telephone sat on an end table, then stopped and looked my way again. "Will you wait here with me?''

I nodded. "You're going to need my help.''

"You seem to know all about what happened to Nedra. I'd be grateful if you'd explain it to me.''

"After you make the calls, Mr. Merchant.''

I sat down on the couch, with the towel-wrapped pistol in my lap, and closed my eyes. Long day, long bad day, and I was bone-tired and I wanted to sleep. Hours to go before I got to do it, though. Hours and miles to go.

Merchant was talking into the phone. I sat there with my eyes shut and tried not to think about the other explanations I would have to make, the ones to Kay and Matt Runyon.

Chapter **23**

KERRY AND I finally had our little showdown on Tuesday evening.

There was another message from her waiting when I got home Monday night, but it was too late and I was too exhausted to return it then. I called her at Bates and Carpenter on Tuesday morning and we arranged for her to come to my place at seven o'clock. It wasn't much of a conversation and it didn't make me feel particularly optimistic; but then, there wasn't anything ominous in her tone and I didn't have any premonitions of doom.

She got there right at seven. We kissed—not much of a kiss —and went into the living room. I asked her if she wanted something to drink; she said no. She drew a deep breath, let it out slowly against her teeth. It made a sound like wind in a hollow place.

"There's something I have to tell you," she said, "and I'd better get right to the point. I haven't been working every night the past couple of weeks. I lied to you about that. I've . . . been seeing someone part of the time. Another man."

"I know."

"I didn't want it to happen, I tried to keep it from—" She stopped as what I'd said kicked in. "You know?"

"Paul Blessing. Blessing Furniture Showrooms."

"My God. How did you . . . ?"

"Barney Rivera. He saw you and Blessing together one night and couldn't wait to tell me."

"How long have you known?"

"Since Friday night, for sure."

"Why didn't you say something?"

"I would have," I said, "if you'd been available."

"You didn't . . . I mean . . ."

"Follow you around? Spy on you? No. I thought about it, but I didn't do it. I didn't want to make something sordid out of it—bad fifties melodrama. I have too much respect for you for that. For myself too."

She was silent for a time. She'd come here to do this a certain way and I'd rocked her equilibrium; she was regrouping.

I asked her, "Do you love him?" It was the question uppermost in my mind and I wanted it out in the open first thing.

"I don't know," she said. "I don't think so, not the way you mean. A strong physical attraction . . . and he's a good man, kind . . ." She let the words trail off. Then, almost angrily, she said, "God, I *hate* this."

"That makes two of us."

"I haven't slept with him. I want you to know that."

"All right."

"I mean it. I haven't."

"I believe you."

"I wanted to, I admit that. I almost did, Saturday night."

"What stopped you?"

"You did. How I feel about you, what we've been to each other. I have too much respect for you too."

"It shouldn't matter, I guess, but it does. I'm glad."

"So am I."

We held eye contact; then we both looked away, as if by mutual consent. It got quiet in there, so quiet I could hear the faint ticking from the old ormolu clock on the mantelpiece. My mother's clock, brought here from Italy nearly one hundred years ago; the lock of my long-dead sister's hair in a yellow envelope was still tucked into the back. Takes a licking and keeps on ticking.

When the silence got to be too loud I said, "So what happens now?"

"I don't know," Kerry said.

"You intend to keep on seeing him?"

"I . . . don't know."

"Which means you want to."

"Part of me does. I can't deny that."

"How about me? Is there a part of you left for me?"

Her eyes had taken on a moist sheen, but at least they were looking at me again. "You think I want to end it between us?"

"Do you?"

"No."

"That's good. Neither do I. But I'm not up to a competition with Blessing for you. I'm too old and too tired and too psychologically beat-up to get into that kind of game. If you want me, fine. If you want him, I'll try to back out as gracefully as I can. But it's got to be one way or the other. No dancing back and forth."

"I wouldn't do that to you."

"Babe," I said, "you already have, for a while now."

She closed her eyes, opened them again. "I know," she said, soft. "I'm sorry. I won't let it go on much longer."

"How long?"

"No more than a few days. Right now I'm confused and ashamed and emotionally screwed-up. I need to get away by myself, somewhere where there's no personal or professional pressure and I can sort out my feelings. Can you accept that?"

"Yes."

"I've already talked to Jim Carpenter. He's letting me have a long weekend off, starting Thursday afternoon."

"Where will you go?"

"No idea. I'll probably just get in the car and drive until I find someplace to stop."

"Call me as soon as you get back?"

"Yes. That's a promise."

There was really nothing more for either of us to say. She stood and I went with her to the door. I said, "Have a safe trip," and she said, "I will. You take care too," and out she went. We didn't kiss and we didn't touch, not even a pat or a hand clasp.

When she was gone I felt all the things I'd felt since Barney Rivera's call: sad, lonely, hurt, needy. But not despondent. The whole business was out in the open finally. And she hadn't slept with Blessing. And she hadn't told me to take a hike, not yet anyway. And there was so much history between us, so many good things. I felt hopeful. Not confident, not secure, just hopeful.

ON WEDNESDAY, Kay Runyon came to see me. She looked better than she had on Monday night, when I'd shattered the last of her illusions about her husband. "Matt and I are coping," she said, and I believed her. She was there to pay me the balance of what she owed me. I told her it wasn't necessary, that I could send a bill later on, but she insisted I figure up my time and expenses and we settle then and there.

I thought I understood why. It was part of a necessary closure for her, a sealing off—as rapidly as possible—from all the recent events and everybody connected with them. Only when that closure was complete could she and her son begin the healing process. When she walked out of there I knew I would never see or hear from her again. And that was as it should be.

She didn't mention her husband's name, not once. Nor did I. I knew, because I'd checked with S.F. General, that he was out of danger, listed in stable condition, expected to recover fully from his gunshot wound. I also knew, from Branislaus, that he had communicated with no one since his admittance to the hospital; had retreated to a place so deep inside himself that no one could reach it. Whether the condition was permanent or not was moot at this point. In any case, there was little question that Victor Runyon had a future date with a mental institution.

ON THURSDAY, I had another visitor—a surprise one this time. Dr. Philip Muncon. He'd come to apologize to me, he said, for his dismissive attitude toward my investigation; and to thank me for helping to save Nedra Merchant's life. Because of his past association with her, he'd been called in as a consultant on her case and he seemed genuinely concerned about her. So we were both guilty of misjudgment. I told him that, and accepted his apology, and shook his hand when he accepted mine.

When I asked him about Nedra's condition, he said he was confident that given enough time she would regain what he termed her "mental equilibrium." How much time? It was impossible to predict; it might take months, even years. And of course there would be scars no matter how long it took—deep emotional scars.

Yes, there would. I knew all about those kinds of scars.

ON FRIDAY, I spoke to Walter Merchant. The police hadn't arrested him Monday night, or since, and the D.A.'s office was still trying to decide if they were going to press charges against him. Not for the shooting—that had been determined to be accidental—but for failure to report it immediately and for leaving the scene with his ex-wife. He didn't think there would be charges. Neither did I.

He'd been to see Nedra, he said, and she had recognized him and spoken briefly to him. He seemed buoyed by this. He badly wanted another chance with her; he intended to do all he could to aid and abet her recovery. He was convinced that what she'd been through would change her, make her realize how dangerously wrong her life-style had been, turn her into a better and more stable person who would be willing to give marriage another try.

He was right that she would be changed. He might not be right that the changes would be for the better, but I didn't tell him that. Let him go on hoping as long as he could. If he was lucky, the things he hoped for might even come true.

AND THEN IT WAS THE WEEKEND, another long, long week-end. I worked a little, puttered a little, drove around a little, read and watched TV a little. And waited. And went on with my own hoping.

What keeps any of us going in this life, when you get right down to it, but hope?

Chapter 24

KERRY CAME BACK ON SUNDAY NIGHT. She didn't call; she showed up unannounced at my flat shortly before nine o'clock. The doorbell rang, jarring me out of a half doze in front of the TV set, and when I went and opened up, there she was. Looking much more composed than she had on Tuesday—well rested and at peace with herself.

"I drove down to Big Sur," she said when we were settled on the couch. "There's nothing like the ocean to help you relax and see things clearly."

"So what did you decide?"

"I decided I'm not going to see Paul Blessing anymore," she said. "But that isn't all. I decided something much more important than that."

"Which is?"

"That you've been right all along. You and Cybil."

"Right about what?"

She took a slow, deep breath, like somebody about to dive off a high board into very cold water. "Do you still want to marry me?" she said.

"Do I . . ." I gawped at her.

"You do, don't you?"

"Well, sure, of course I do."

"Then I accept."

"You mean you . . . you're willing to—"

"Not just willing—I *want* to marry you. Tomorrow, next month, whenever. I love you. I love you and I don't want to be with anybody else and I don't know why I thought I did."

I didn't say anything. I couldn't say anything. I just sat there grinning at her like a fool.